THE LAST
TABOO

Living with Death

Dominic McGinley

MENTOR

This Edition first published 2000 by

MENTOR BOOKS
43 Furze Road,
Sandyford Industrial Estate,
Dublin 18.

Tel. (01) 295 2112/3   Fax. (01) 295 2114
e-mail: admin@mentorbooks.ie
website: www.mentorbooks.ie

ISBN: 1-947548-86-6

A catalogue record for this book is available
from the British Library

Disclaimer
Neither the publisher nor the author can accept
responsibility for actions taken as a result of consulting
this publication. Those who wish to take advice or to
undertake counselling on any matter affecting them
should contact a suitably qualified professional advisor
or counsellor. It is always adviseable to ask for the
credentials of the professional whom you are consulting.
All information regarding costs are accurate at the time
of publication. Interested parties may contact the author
through the publishers regarding updates of information
presented.

Typesetting, editing, design and layout by
MENTOR BOOKS
Cover photograph courtesy of Slidefile

Printed in Ireland by ColourBooks

1 3 5 7 9 10 8 6 4 2

To all my family, with love.

Acknowledgements

The Last Taboo could never have been written without all the help and encouragement I received from my wife, Moya. She was my stalwart supporter from the time I first mooted this book until the very last full stop was placed. She provided tremendous support – encouraging me, typing text, and making the many pots of tea which sustained me through research, writing and re-writing. I can't thank her enough! Thanks also to my children Catherine, Dominic and Sarah, who provided insightful comments and critique and supported the project in spite of the unusual subject.

I greatly appreciate the help of all of those for whom death is not taboo, who willingly provided information and offered clarification on many points. To my brother Hugh, who provided insight into the work of the emergency services. To George Murphy who gave me information about coffin-makers, embalmers, undertakers and the processes of burial and cremation; also to Ray Hennessey and Keith Massey and Anne Cummins.

Sincere thanks to Dr Brian J Farrell, Dublin City Coroner, for his time, interest and support; and to his staff, especially Brian Hanney, manager at the Coroner's Office. Thanks to Professor William Stanley Monkhouse, head of the Anatomy Department at the Royal College of Surgeons, Dublin, for the benefit of his wisdom, experience and objectivity; also to his colleague Eric Clarke for his courtesy and helpfulness. Thanks too to Professor C. Meban of the Anatomy Department at Queens University, Belfast.

Thanks to the Insurance Corporation of Ireland, to the Probate Office, to the Solicitors' Bar Association, to the Central Statistics Office and other professional bodies who provided information and clarification. To the Irish Hospice Foundation, Barnardo's, the Irish Sudden Infant Death Association and The Samaritans for their help, a very big thank you.

Last, but not least, I wish to express my gratitude to all those who have been bereaved in various ways and who were willing to talk and share with me their experiences and feelings about their loved ones, in spite of their considerable sadness. Thank you all!

Contents

Introduction

Human life, as we know it, is a relatively recent phenomenon, appearing on the earth just over one and a half million years ago. In that comparatively short time the human race has come a long way. The evolution of a thinking, sentient being, capable of a wide range of emotions, of complex thought and action, is that which sets humans apart from other species.

Yet, there is one thing we share with other species. We must die. We know and understand this, yet many of us tend to live in conscious denial of this simple fact. Life is wonderful and sweet and sad and hard and tragic and painful and joyful and remarkable, but inevitably short and finite. Everyone has their own answer as to the meaning of life, and the remarkable thing is that we are all right and we are all wrong, because nobody actually knows.

We must all face death some day. Everyone of us, at some time or another, will be faced with the death of someone we love. That death, whether it be of a partner, a parent, a child, a friend or a close family member, will disrupt the pattern of our life and of those around us. For those who believe in an afterlife, death is the end of our physical life and the beginning of a new, spiritual existence. For others it is simply the end.

Most of us, at some time or another, will need the help of the medical profession in the person of doctors and nurses. Many others will have to avail of the emergency services. We often take for granted the daily heroism shown by our medics, police, ambulance and fire personnel. The dedicated work of air, sea and land rescue teams is also underestimated. They all deal with death on a regular basis. Very often they encounter death in the most distressing, gruesome and tragic circumstances and face situations we could hardly imagine.

The Last Taboo is a book about death, but it is not a morbid book. Nor is it a sentimental book. **The Last Taboo** is about the issues relating to death which many people tend to avoid. There are practical, social and legal issues about death and its aftermath which are worth looking at while we are in good health, so that if someone we love dies, then we shall be better prepared for the pain and trauma involved.

> We do not have to wait for the painful death of someone close to us or the shock of terminal illness to force us into looking at our lives. Nor are we condemned to go out empty-handed at death to meet the unknown. We can begin, here and now, to find meaning in our lives. We can make every moment an opportunity to change and to prepare – wholeheartedly, precisely, and with peace of mind – for death and eternity.
>
> [Quoted from:
> *The Tibetan Book of Living and Dying*
> by Sogyal Rinpoche]

CHAPTER 1

The bereavement process

How do we grieve?

On Death and Dying, by the renowned author Dr Elizabeth Kübler–Ross, was the first book to clearly identify the stages of bereavement. These stages may include, in any order, loneliness and sadness, numbness, shock, anger, guilt, disbelief, despair and hopelessness, anxiety, fear, depression, longing, relief. There may also be many physical reactions affecting sleep, appetite, energy, concentration as well as general aches and pains in the body. This study of the dying – thanatology – was considered taboo even in medical circles until Dr Kübler–Ross dedicated herself to it. Her reasoning for taking on such a subject was that she thought it peculiar that a society capable of putting a man on the the moon had 'never put any effort into the definition of human death'.

It was then realised that those who are dying, and those who are grieving, follow virtually the same pattern of dealing with their situation, and that this area of study was not only legitimate, but necessary. Medical schools worldwide are now recognising the need to include bereavement as a subject in their curricula.

Numbness, shock, disbelief and denial

Usually the first aspect of grief is a sense of numbness, shock and disbelief. There is often a sense of unreality. Some describe the feeling as 'like being wrapped in cotton wool' or 'like swimming underwater'. Most people respond to bad news, even when the facts are clear, by saying: 'I can't believe it!' or 'This can't be happening!' or in the words of Willy Russell's song from the musical *Blood Brothers*: 'Tell me it's not true!' Poor concentration is normal when we are numbed by grief.

Emotional conflict

When a bereavement is unexpected, as with the sudden death of a family member due to an accident or an illness, the grief reaction is usually very strong indeed. There can be an element of conflict or guilt in this kind of grief, however, especially if there were unresolved issues between the deceased and the grievers. If, for example, a parent was alcoholic or abusive, the spouse and children might find it particularly difficult to come to terms with their loss. This could be because their sense of loyalty to the person who has died conflicts with their sense of relief that the source of much of their stress has suddenly gone. The grief reaction is also very intense if there has been an over-dependence on the dead person and it may take a considerable time before those who are grieving can rationalise their loss.

Anger

Another aspect of grief may be a strong feeling of anger.

Many people get angry that such a thing should happen to them or to their loved one: 'Why me?' They may get angry with God or with the loved one who is dying or who has died: 'How could they do this to me?' or 'It's not fair!' Those who are supporting the bereaved, such as friends or neighbours, may themselves become the focus of the bereaved person's anger, which can be distressing for the carers. In time, however, the angry reaction usually subsides.

Those who find themselves in a supporting role frequently try to bring an 'emotional band-aid' to the situation. There are no ready-made solutions and those who are grieving must be allowed to grieve, to go through the whole painful process themselves — in their own way! Sigmund Freud called this 'grief work' and we all have to do our own grief work in our own time.

Seamus Heaney captured a sense of this emotion in his poem *Mid-Term Break,* where he describes his mother's grief on the death of his younger brother: '. . . as my mother coughed out angry tearless sighs . . .' The important thing, however, as the psychologist Geoffrey Gorer put it, is that: 'mourning should not be treated as a weakness!' Another common reaction to grief may be a child-like belief that if one changes one's lifestyle in some way, or promises to be a better person, that somehow events can be changed.

Pining and searching
Those who are bereaved may have the experience of 'seeing' their loved one in a crowd or in the distance.

This is part of a searching which we go through when we are coming to terms with our loss. There is a yearning within us to see the person again, alive and well. We miss them deeply and pine after them when we are awake and even in our sleep. Dreams of the dead loved one are very common and our imagination can conjure ghostly images of them too.

Patrick Kavanagh wrote a beautifully moving poem *In Memory of My Father,* after his father died, in which he reveals: '. . . Every old man I see reminds me of my father when he had fallen in love with death, one time when sheaves were gathered . . .'

Depression

Another stage of the grieving process is depression. This is often a reflection of anger or guilt, and can last a very long time. Having the opportunity to relive the events surrounding the death can be immensely therapeutic. While friends and family usually provide a listening ear, in other cases short-term prescribed medication can prove extremely useful. Many bereaved people experience feelings of choking or breathlessness, insomnia, lack of appetite or nausea, poor concentration or forgetfulness, among other symptoms. In some cases overdependence on drugs or alcohol can develop during the time of bereavement.

Guilt

The guilt felt by some bereaved people about the death of someone close may stem from a failure to visit the person before they died, or from anxiety over an unresolved conflict with the dead person. Another reason for feelings of guilt may be a sense that if they had called or phoned the person when they said they would, that the circumstances which led to the deceased's death might never have arisen. When guilt is a factor, the bereaved cannot be cajoled through their feelings. It may take some time before such issues are fully and appropriately resolved. This is why individual or group bereavement counselling can be of immense benefit.

It is also quite common for family members to fall out with each other because of unresolved issues before, during or after the funeral. It is not an admission of failure to ask for the help of a skilled counsellor; rather it is a very positive step which bereaved people can take in order to help themselves recover their normal, positive outlook on life.

Signs and symbols
The bereaved usually carry out a variety of symbolic acts in their time of grief. Poring over old photographs, going to the cemetery or visiting favourite places where their loved one used to go, preparing favourite meals and even setting the person's place at the table, are among some examples. Holding on to clothes or treasured mementos of the deceased or wearing a piece of clothing or jewellery belonging to the dead person are common too. These keepsakes can give great comfort and a sense of the presence of the deceased. Sometimes these signs and symbols are difficult for others to

fathom and the challenge for carers is to be sensitive to the needs of the bereaved.

Comforting beliefs

It is well recognised that those who have a religious or spiritual faith which is integrated into their daily lives, find immense comfort in their beliefs at a time of grief. They may well be able to reconcile themselves to loss sooner than those who don't have a specific religious or spiritual practice. The main world religions have rituals associated with death which have the power to be very comforting and therapeutic.

Dying of a broken heart

It sometimes happens, however, that a bereaved person simply cannot overcome his or her grief. The person's health suffers and he or she can find no reason to go on living. Effectively the bereaved person may lose the will to live in the absence of the deceased and may die of a broken heart not long after the death of a loved one.

Acceptance and re-adjustment

Often the most difficult emotion to express in the bereavement process is acceptance, and it may take up to a year or more before a person becomes fully reconciled to their loss. The bereaved person eventually re-adjusts and regains his or her natural optimism, and life becomes worth living again. For some the process is completed sooner than others. Everyone's rate of acceptance is different and friends of the bereaved may need to be very patient.

Counsellors recognise three tasks which must be completed before the bereaved recovers. First is the **intellectual acceptance** of the loss. This acceptance may involve viewing the dead body or even preparing the corpse for burial, organising the funeral or participating in the ceremony, or perhaps even choosing the readings or music. Any or all of these activities can be most helpful.

The second task is the **emotional acceptance** of the loss – coming to terms with one's real feelings and living through the pain of loss.

The third task involves **reorganising** one's life and developing a sense of identity separate from the one who has died. As Geoffrey Gorer put it '. . . one must find a new way of seeing oneself.' Some may find this task extremely difficult, especially if they were always seen by others in terms of their partner's occupation, as in 'the teacher's wife'.

Getting it together

The reorganising tasks for the bereaved may include re-discovering old talents or finding new ones, like learning to drive or becoming computer-literate. It will be necessary to look back over the relationship, to understand its significance in the light of one's personal philosophy and to come to terms with a new reality – without the departed loved one. Professor John Hinton, in his book *Dying*, says: 'Mourning cannot be complete unless the bereaved succeed in making an adequate worldly adjustment without the one they have lost.'

When the bereaved reach this stage they have reached a mental and emotional (and often spiritual) acceptance of their loss and the dead person is 'present' in their thoughts in a more natural way. The grieving process is complete, although the sense of loss never goes away.

CHAPTER 2

Children and death

What do children know about death?

It has been estimated that by the time they are six years old, children in Ireland have seen more than a thousand deaths on television. These will, of course, be mostly related to dramatic representations, films and cartoons. These deaths, while occasionally quite graphic, do not generally impinge on children's reality, although they have the capacity to disturb.

The emotions evoked by drama mimic our real emotions and some of the memories we have of, say, the death of Bambi's mother in the Disney cartoon, or the final moments of ET's time on earth can bring us to tears. It is interesting, though, that humans are the only creatures capable of deliberately placing themselves in a situation of either sadness or fear. Precisely why we choose to do so is, perhaps, another of the great mysteries of our humanity.

Our attitudes to, and perceptions of, death and its consequences are formed within the family. In Europe and America in past centuries, before the current understanding of childhood was developed, children were treated like mini-adults. Many homes would have a *memento mori* or reminder of death. This might be a picture portraying a death scene or indeed an apparently innocent scene which on closer inspection showed a skull hidden by way of a *trompe l'oeil* (from the French 'to deceive the eye').

Children's reading was usually scripture based and, because of high mortality rates among the young, great emphasis was placed on death and the afterlife. It was also considered appropriate by some for children to be shown the gibbeted bodies of executed criminals in order to deter the young ones from a life of crime. Such 'in-your-face' approaches would not be tolerated today.

Real death, as opposed to dramatic representations, however, has a different sense to it. The emotions evoked by the death of a loved one or of a beloved pet run deeper and longer. They have a much more profound effect on us than the temporary emotions we experience by listening to stories, watching movies, looking at television or reading. It is seen as acceptable to have a little weep at the demise of Romeo and Juliet, but when the death is for real, the emotional consequences, as well as the practical ones last much, much longer.

Talking about death

It may be because we are unsure of the pattern of grief that we tend to avoid discussing death-evoked emotions. The uncertainty we feel when dealing with the real and long-lasting grief of others may also cause us, as carers, to avoid altogether the one who is grieving; simply because we don't know what to say. We may fear that speaking to the bereaved adult or child in a particular way will cause them to be tearful or upset, leaving us confused or embarrassed or feeling guilty for having provoked such a reaction.

Death is a great mystery and adults often underestimate the need to talk with children about the subject. If a child's need for simple, accurate, age-appropriate information is ignored, then the child can experience unnecessary confusion. It is important to give children a proper vocabulary. Do use words like shroud, embalming, cremation, interment and obituary. Don't be afraid to explain to children what these words mean.

Children go through much the same process of bereavement as adults. It is incorrect, therefore, to assume that if you say nothing to children about death that they will simply get over it. A child who is not told why everyone around them is upset or why a loved one has gone away, may come to his or her own conclusions. The adage: 'what they don't know, they make up' applies, often leading children to have exaggerated and avoidable fears.

Fear of being buried alive

Many people have a terror of being buried alive. During Victorian times the fear of being buried alive was so common that elaborate signalling systems for connecting the dead person's finger to the outside world were often used. If the person woke up in their coffin they could then attract the attention of someone to let them know that they were still alive.

In earlier times, when sailors were buried at sea, the final stitch in the shroud was sewn by the captain of the ship. He was also required to pierce the tip of the nose of the deceased with the needle to establish that the person was really dead. Even with modern medical diagnosis such fears of being buried alive remain common. Children who have such fears need gentle reassurance. It is worth remembering that an embalmed body could not possibly re-animate because the blood has been removed.

Bereavement in children

Bereavement in children may appear to take a shorter time than in adults. A child's attention span is shorter than that of an adult and consequently youngsters may not be as absorbed by grief as the grown-ups around them. That is not to say that children are not affected by death. They are, but in a child-like way. As with adults, their pattern of grieving is quite predictable, although individual variations will occur.

Children at a funeral will usually play quite happily with each other after the solemn moments and, depending on their age, may only react tearfully to the apparent distress of those around them. The way the adults express their emotions, however, will have a direct bearing on how the children express their own feelings.

It is important to stress to children that a good cry can be very therapeutic. It is generally considered unwise to suppress one's need in this area. A 'stiff upper-lip' approach to grief, which many people feel obliged to adopt, is not to be recommended. After all, tears are merely salt water containing other trace elements, and a 'good bawl' is a marvellous way to relieve pent-up emotions.

Emotional triggers

Grief can surface in various ways. We can never know what will spark a sudden outpouring of grief. Expressing our emotions openly is nothing to be ashamed of. Accepting such a response as normal is a healthy part of the grieving process. Everyone experiences mixed and conflicting emotions following the death of a loved one. Sympathetic adults and teenagers can help even very young children to cope with loss. Reassurance and comfort will always help too.

CHAPTER 3

Children and grief

How can we help grieving children?

A number of organisations are involved in providing counselling services for children. **Barnardo's** have a well-developed programme for helping bereaved children and have produced a very useful pamphlet which is full of practical advice.

Sólás, in Irish, means 'comfort' or 'solace'. It is also the name of the national counselling service provided by Barnardo's. They offer information and advice; family, individual and group counselling and advice and training for groups working with bereaved children. In addition they have a library information service, which gives information on all aspects of bereavement and childcare.

A new community-based counselling service for children at primary school level has recently come on stream. It is known as **Rainbows**. Many of those involved are teachers and in some cases the local school is the centre used for group work. The counselling group for post-primary level is called **Spectrum** and the group for adults is called **Prism**.

Another group of teachers have become involved in the counselling area under the heading **TACA**, which means 'support' in Irish. The acronym stands for

Teachers Adopting Counselling Approaches. TACA provides education and training for teachers who wish to further their skills and their understanding of children's needs in terms of bereavement, as well as other forms of counselling. The Hospice Movement also provides specialised counselling services for children.

The benefits of discussion

There are very definite benefits in discussing death with children. If we adopt a sensible and sensitive approach children will learn a deep respect for life; that life is meaningful and precious and really worth living. Proper terminology will help them understand the feelings associated with bereavement and reduce their fears. By helping children to deal with suffering and sorrow, loss and death, we can help them to grow in maturity.

A simple, early acknowledgement of our mortality serves a useful purpose in preparing us for what is to come. Many Irish children are taught prayers which include the idea of death. Most children know the night prayer:

> *Now I lay me down to sleep,*
> *I pray the Lord my soul to keep.*
> *If I should die before I wake,*
> *I pray the Lord my soul to take.*

Death Education

Some schools in the United States have introduced a module which deals specifically with death. These programmes are designed to help children to develop self-knowledge and coping skills and are run in conjunction with parents, teachers and local clergy. The children learn to explore issues of loss and to develop coping strategies. They also learn to understand how they can support others and be supported by their peers. What this programme is doing is reintroducing the community element of grieving, something which has been lost over time because of the changes in the way society works.

It is worth noting that religious education programmes in Irish primary schools are designed, in part, to assist children in their early exploration of the meaning of life. The aim is to help them to face up to, and learn from, painful experiences which they may encounter as they go through life. Topics for discussion are fear and loss, suffering and death and other aspects of life.

Religious education programmes in some primary schools include a section in the teacher's manual which deals with death. If a tragedy occurs which affects all the children, it may be necessary to have a class discussion or even a whole school discussion, This tragedy may involve the death of a child, or the death of an adult who is known to many or all of the children. Naturally, the utmost sensitivity is required in order to avoid generating a morbid fear of death among the children.

Most post-primary schools also offer well-developed religious education programmes which challenge the students to examine important life (and death) issues from a denominational point of view. These programmes have the capacity to help young people to clarify their values and to understand the attitudes of the different churches to moral issues. The recent introduction of a Social, Personal and Health Education (SPHE) module in primary and post-primary schools also acknowledges the need to discuss the whole human life-cycle — from 'womb to tomb'.

Rehearsing grief

When a child's pet dies, for example, it is most important to allow the child to grieve and to mourn. Burying the pet with appropriate ceremony may prove very helpful. Tears for the lost loved one should be accepted and encouraged. Children who are not allowed to grieve appropriately for such minor losses will find it very difficult to grieve properly when greater losses occur. Unfortunately, in our society, boys are often discouraged from expressing their grief, for example 'big boys don't cry', while girls are often allowed, and even expected, to show more emotion.

There is a danger that we may fall into the trap of patronising children about death. It makes no sense to replace a dead goldfish and expect the child to be satisfied with clearly untrue arguments about the goldfish having changed overnight. Honesty is certainly the best policy when talking to children about death. It is essential for children to realise that adults don't have all of the answers all of the time. On the other hand, brutal frankness, however well-intentioned, is just as inappropriate as avoiding the issue altogether.

The 'what ifs' and 'if onlys' are really very important too, as they can help the child to come to terms with any guilt or anger they might feel about the event. Adults can then help the child to recognise appropriate and inappropriate guilt and to put those feelings into proper context. Being told that 'there's nothing that can be done, so get on with it', is rarely of any comfort.

Name it

Naming feelings for children and allowing them to express them can be very helpful; saying things like: 'You're very sad at the moment. Tell me about your Granny. What was her name? How did she die? Do you miss her?'

Be patient if the child is shy about expressing his or her feelings. Children, like adults, are sometimes embarrassed about revealing how they feel. It is useful to seek advice if a child appears not to grieve at all. This can be a sign that he or she has not accepted the death and is in denial. In this case professional help may be required.

Levels of understanding

Up to the time they begin primary school, children tend to see death as reversible. Watching cartoons on television tends to confirm this in very young minds. Children will often play at pretending to be dead. They lie on the ground and say: 'I'm dead!' and then they jump up laughing, and say: 'I'm alive again!' It is evident that death is not a clearly defined reality for many younger children.

By the time they are in third class (eight or nine years old) children see death more realistically. There is a sense that all living things must die, but they don't tend to take it personally. They may well imagine that they can control death and perhaps even avoid it by being clever.

Young children can be very literal in their interpretation of things adults say about death. It is not helpful, therefore, for adults to use phrases like 'He's gone to sleep' or 'She's gone to a better place.' The child may then want to know why the loved one won't wake up or even ask to be brought to the 'better place'. One young child wanted to join in the search when he overheard his aunt say that she had 'lost a baby'!

From about the age of ten onwards the reality and permanence of death begins to sink in, and children may even suffer from nightmares and anxiety about death. Dr. Anthony Clare has observed that 'real loss of innocence is not a child's discovery of sex, but of death, of his or her own mortality'.

Including children in the grieving process
Many believe that it is very important to include children when a death occurs within the family. It is decidedly unhelpful, especially if the children are closely related to the deceased, to exclude them from the proceedings. They might be encouraged to write a farewell letter, make a card or place some small token into the coffin to acknowledge their feelings of sadness and loss, and to realise that death is a changed state; different from life. If it is a child who has died, then

young brothers, sisters, cousins and friends need much reassurance about their own position within the family. Not including children in the bereavement process can have the effect of stirring inappropriate feelings of anxiety and guilt. If a child shows reservations about viewing the body, then that should be respected. In certain cultures children were forced to kiss dead relatives goodbye. Children can be greatly traumatised by forcing them to do this.

It is important to trust children if they say they don't want even to touch the dead person. After all, death is cold and it can be quite shocking to realise just how cold a corpse can be. Many adults find the thought of touching or kissing a dead body repugnant, so it's not surprising that children might feel the same. It is important to explain to children beforehand that a dead person feels cold to the touch. Explain why in simple terms (see Chapter 10 When We Die) and allow them to decide whether or not they want to touch the corpse.

Visiting the cemetery
Visiting the cemetery to see where a loved one is buried can be very comforting for children as well as adults. It is possible for us to communicate with a strong memory of the deceased person and it can be a valuable source of psychological relief. Visit any cemetery and you will see individuals and families working through their grief by tidying or beautifying a loved one's grave. Children should be offered the opportunity to be involved. Birthdays, anniversaries and other special occasions prompt graveyard visits and it is amazing to see just

how many people turn up for the ceremonies which are carried out on Cemetery Sunday every May. These are rituals of powerful significance, both spiritually and psychologically.

If cremation is chosen, it is most important to explain to children that the dead person can feel no pain.

Teenagers thoughts on death

Some teenagers go through a phase of being intrigued by death — when they have a fascination for horror stories, witchcraft, ghost stories and other stories about death. Television, video films and fiction in the horror genre are the staple entertainment of many youngsters of this age. For others their religious and spiritual thinking is developing beyond the magical stage and there is a greater need to discuss these matters in a serious way at home and at school. Without help, morbid thoughts can remain uppermost in the young person's mind for much longer than necessary. The insecurity generated by the sudden death of a parent, sibling or peer, can be very great indeed.

Within the family circle, teenagers will need to be included in discussions about roles within the family. It is essential to avoid putting inappropriate responsibility on a bereaved youngster. The support of the peer group will be very important at this time. Just being there for each other is often enough and silent company may be exactly what the bereaved person needs.

What can we do?

We must accept that children will need truthful answers to help them to come to terms with their loss. We ourselves may find this distressing, but children deserve to be told the facts as simply as possible and to be included in the whole grieving process. Suggestions are:

- Children should be told of the death by someone familiar. They need the comfort of a trusted adult.
- Simple terms like 'dying' and 'dead' should be used, avoiding euphemisms like 'lost' or 'gone away' or 'gone to heaven'.
- Explain what dead actually means, that the person cannot feel any pain and that while they might look like they are asleep, they aren't and cannot wake up.
- Allow children to express any emotions in whatever way they choose, e.g. anger, tears, withdrawing etc.
- Don't be afraid to pray with children. It can help if prayers are said for the person who has died and for those who are left behind. Formal or informal prayers will do.
- Don't be afraid to allow children see you openly expressing your own emotions.
- Expect to have to repeat explanations.
- Be available to answer questions and freely admit that you haven't got all the answers.
- Reassure children and build their self-esteem, while being supportive and listening intuitively.
- It may be useful for children to make a card, to write a letter to the deceased or to draw a picture. This may or may not be put into or on the coffin.

- They might also choose a memento to put in the coffin or select a keepsake of the person.
- Make suitable reading material available for children.
- Explain in simple terms how a dead person looks and allow children to decide if they want to view the body or not.
- Having given children appropriate information about what happens at a funeral, allow them to decide whether or not to attend.
- Allowing the children to participate in the funeral ceremony can be most helpful.
- Try to keep children as close to their usual routine as possible.
- Be aware that children may suffer from vague, non-specific aches and pains after a significant loss and they may also find it difficult to return to school after a bereavement.
- Explain that other children can be quite insensitive and may make inappropriate comments. Adults can be insensitive too.
- Be aware that sometimes when bereaved, children regress, reverting to earlier childish and clingy behaviour.
- Allow for good and bad days and apparently unexplained temper tantrums or tearfulness.
- Accept that children, with the love and support of those around them, should eventually come to terms with their loss.
- Be patient, but if children appear to be grieving too much or not at all, then consult your GP.

CHAPTER 4

Care of the dying

Impending death

The news that someone you love and care for has a terminal illness can be absolutely devastating. Knowing the stages of bereavement does nothing to lessen the dreadful shock of learning that someone who is unwell will soon be dead. Anticipatory grief, which is anxiety about the future suffering and death of the patient, is inevitable.

It is not unusual for those who are dying and for their family and friends to skirt around the issue of impending death. Each is afraid to upset the other and so no one says anything. Human nature is complex and there are unspoken signals which people tend to give when they do not want to be told that an illness is terminal. This goes for both patient and family. Denial of the obvious reality of inevitable death is very common. Some doctors lack tact, however, and an insensitive approach to either patient or family can add unnecessarily to their burden.

Studies have shown that those who are dying, even children, usually know the truth of their situation. They may even try to put a brave face on things in order to spare their family and friends worry. Medical professionals agree that there can be great benefits to both patient and family in coming to terms with the reality of the situation early on. Even tacit acknowledgement of the facts can allow the dying person to get their affairs in order if they haven't already done so, and enable them to die with serenity and dignity.

Nowadays, with the advanced clinical skills of the medical profession few terminal diagnoses are wrong. It must be said, though, that temporary remission in the case of certain diseases is relatively common. Remission gives hope and buys the patient and their family and friends more time. Then when the inevitable happens, those left behind usually have very positive memories of their deceased loved one because they have had the chance to become closer. Although for others that extra time makes parting all the harder to bear. There is always the added hope that a miraculous cure will occur. Such events are rare, although they do happen.

Hospice care

The English doctor Dame Cicely Saunders began **The Hospice Movement** in St Christopher's, in Sydenham, England, in 1967. Her aim was to promote dying with dignity, arguing that death is not a medical failure, rather it is part of the natural process of living. She promoted the idea of appropriate care and support for the dying with a view to providing the best quality of life that was possible.

She pioneered the notion of palliative care which gives the dying effective pain control, so that they can live relatively painlessly to the end. She has received many awards for her work and for her writing on *Care of the Dying* and *Management of Terminal Illness*.

The Irish Hospice Foundation (IHF) was founded as a result of the dedication of Dr Mary Redmond. Her vision for the Hospice in Ireland is that palliative care should be available for all who need it. In the tenth anniversary publication from the IHF, Dr Redmond states that 'no one who is terminally ill should have to suffer chronic pain.'

Echoing the sentiments of the original Hospice Movement, the philosophy of the hospice in Ireland is: 'the care of the dying demands all we can do to enable patients to live fully until they die.'

Essential elements in the work of the IHF include the process of educating professionals and the public to the work of the hospice and the provision of appropriate training in palliative care for those who work with terminally ill patients in hospital or in the patient's own home. The IHF identifies needs and encourages the establishment of independent services. One significant element in their fund-raising activities is that money raised locally for hospice facilities is used locally.

Palliative care

Palliative care for the terminally ill is now a recognised medical discipline. Previously it was available only to those suffering from the painful effects of cancer. Now, however, palliative care is available to anyone who is terminally ill. It is a personalised regime of medication which provides maximum pain relief while leaving the patient capable and in control of their daily routine. It is envisioned as total care for the patient and also includes working with the family. It is dedicated to the physical, mental, psychological and spiritual welfare of clients, 'adding life to days if not days to life'.

Soul pain

In his book *Mortally Wounded*, Michael Kearney, consultant in palliative care in Our Lady's Hospice and St. Vincent's Hospital, Dublin refers to 'soul pain'. This is the deep emotional, psychological and spiritual distress which can be experienced by those who are dying.

Physical pain is often exacerbated by emotional pain and anything that can be employed to ease both is to be welcomed. Psychotherapy is often used to assist terminally-ill patients. Many gain significantly from discussions with a spiritual advisor and can acquire a sense of peace in spite of their suffering.

Michael Kearney observes that those involved professionally with the care of the dying have come to see that family and friends are very important to the patient's well-being during the final stages of the illness. They can help to ease the deep anguish which many dying people experience. Many of the old Irish sayings contain more than a germ of truth: *'Is faoi scáth a chéile a mhaireann na ndaoine* – People live within the shelter of each other.'

Other services

Research is another key factor in hospice work. Studies are ongoing into the use of morphine in pain-control regimes and into a greater understanding of the expectations for the quality of life of the terminally ill. Another area of study for the IHF is how bereavement affects individuals and families and how they can benefit from suitable counselling services.

AIDS

There has been an increase in the number of AIDS patients in Ireland. While there are four beds for terminally-ill AIDS patients in Our Lady's Hospital in Harold's Cross, Dublin, the Regional Hospital in Laois has recently been designated as a national centre for the treatment of HIV sufferers. Training courses for specialised HIV nursing are ongoing at the centre.

HEBER is the Association For Hospital And Allied Bereavement Groups in Ireland. The IHF provides for the administration and development of the work of HEBER. It also provides advice and support for individuals or groups who wish to become involved in bereavement counselling.

In previous generations most people died at home in their own beds. In recent times, however, the majority of people die in a hospital or in a nursing home. One aspect of the home care provided by the hospice teams is that it facilitates people who wish to die in their own homes. They can spend their last days and hours in comfortable, familiar surroundings.

Dying at home

In an article in the *Irish Medical Times* Dr Brigid Maher wrote: '. . . if a person is going to die, they should be given the option to die at home . . . as there is an intimacy that can only exist at home. Families can sit and talk and pray together as a loved one fades away. There is a unity in the grief.'

In Ireland, in times gone by, people prayed for 'the grace of a happy death'. To die in familiar surroundings, in the company of those you love and having gone through the stages of acceptance, forgiveness and reconciliation with as little pain as possible, would indeed bring a sense of fulfilment and completion to one's final act — the transition from this world to the next. The ancients called this *ars moriendi,* or the art of dying well, something we all might wish for.

Joseph Sharp, chaplain to terminally-ill patients at a Dallas hospital, observed in his book *Living Our Dying* that the 'bond of intimacy is often strengthened and intensified when one is dealing with the dying'. Many people would echo this sentiment, saying that they grew extremely close, closer than they had ever been before, to a dying relative, simply by being there.

To those who are involved in the care of the dying (especially professional carers) Joseph Sharp advises them: 'not to allow their knowledge of the stages through which dying people go, to numb them to the reality of death or to how the dying person is at any given moment'.

The Natural Death Centre
In the UK a non-profit charitable project called **The Natural Death Centre** was initiated in 1991. Their main aims are to support those dying at home, to

support their carers and to assist in arranging suitable funerals, but they also aim to help to improve the 'quality of dying'. They have produced a number of handbooks and leaflets including *The Natural Death Handbook*. They also have information on 'living wills' (*see* page 61).

CHAPTER 5

When a child dies

Losing a child

The death of anyone evokes sadness and loss, but the death of a child is immensely traumatic. Parents feel that they should never have to bury a child, but it sometimes happens. In Ireland children are less likely to die of illness than they are to die by accident, although certain congenital birth defects do reduce the life expectancy of some children.

The greatest loss for parents when a child dies is, perhaps, the loss of potential. They will never know what might have been, what kind of person that precious child might have become. It can take a very long time to come to terms with that depth of loss. Again the comfort of those around us, including those who have shared a similar experience, can be of immense solace.

In Ireland at the turn of the century the death rate among infants under one year was about 140 out of 1,000. In 1977 the rate was almost 16 per 1,000. Happily the current rate is less than 6 per 1,000 live births, a rate which clearly indicates the high quality of our maternity care and medical services.

Miscarriage, stillbirth and neo-natal death

According to Dr A R Scialli, MD for Georgetown University Medical Centre, miscarriage is 'a distressing but common event that usually occurs from natural errors in early embryo development'. He also identifies less common factors such as maternal age, hormone levels and immune system function as well as longterm exposure to tobacco, caffeine and alcohol. Certain prescription drugs may also precipitate miscarriage. For some women recurring miscarriage becomes a distressing aspect of their fertile years. Because miscarriage was relatively common in the past, very little emphasis was put on the feelings and grief of couples over the loss of a hoped-for child. This lack of sensitivity is no longer evident today and couples who lose their baby during the early stages of pregnancy are offered much help and support.

Stillbirth is when a baby is born dead. This occurence is now recognised as an even more traumatic event than miscarriage. Thankfully medical knowledge has increased to a point where stillbirths are more rare. When a stillbirth does happen parents are encouraged to see their dead baby, to acknowledge their loss and to take time with their child after the birth. They may choose to name their baby before making funeral arrangements. The registration of a stillbirth is now quite a common procedure.

Newborn or neonatal deaths usually occur between three and twenty-eight days of birth while cot deaths may occur up to eighteen months after birth. Continuing research into possible causes of sudden infant death has helped towards a much greater understanding of such tragedies. Studies have shown possible links between sudden infant death and parents smoking, the baby's sleeping position or even long-haul air travel.

Every year in Ireland several hundred babies die soon after birth. Future research will obviously reduce the risks to newborn babies even more. Doctors are continually perfecting techniques for sustaining the lives of even very premature babies, but realistically it will never be possible to eliminate all risks. In the developed world, infant mortality is at an extremely low level. Knowing this, however, does nothing to lessen the tragedy for those whose baby has died — at whatever stage.

Organisations such as the **Irish Stillbirth and Neonatal Death Society** (ISANDS) and **Irish Sudden Infant Death Association** (ISIDA) have trained volunteers and counsellors who can provide tremendous comfort and support for grieving parents. Their members have already experienced the grief and trauma of sudden infant or neonatal death themselves. ISANDS have also produced an excellent booklet called *A Little Lifetime* for bereaved parents and their families. They also have a leaflet prepared specially for those whose baby died some time ago.

Registering the baby

For some, acknowledgement of their baby's short life is made more complete by registering their baby (within forty-two days) and carrying out a funeral service with burial in either the 'Holy Angels' plot or the family plot in their local cemetery. Annual memorial ceremonies are organised by both of the above organisations. These provide an opportunity for bereaved parents and relatives to acknowledge their loss and to celebrate the gift of their baby's short life.

The loss of a baby through miscarriage, stillbirth or sudden infant death may be a couple's first encounter with the reality of death. This can have a devastating effect on the relationship as the father and the mother of the deceased child tend to grieve differently.

Blame and guilt

Self-blame is a common feeling among grieving parents. Anyone who may have been responsible for minding the seemingly healthy infant may become the focus of a couple's anger, which can be especially distressing for the carer, who is entirely innocent of blame.

Other children in the family can be profoundly disturbed by their own sense of loss and also by the grief of their parents. They may also feel significant guilt and depression because they may have resented the attention given to the new baby. They will need extra love and reassurance that they are in no way responsible for their sibling's death.

It is essential for all – parents, grandparents, children and other relatives – to acknowledge the way in which the grieving process disrupts the family unit and to understand that grief is the primary way in which humans deal with loss.

CHAPTER 6

Abortion

Attitudes to abortion

At present, the right to life of the unborn child is enshrined in the Irish Constitution and one can always expect a strong emotional reaction to the issue. It is very easy to make sweeping generalisations about the rights and wrongs of abortion; whether or not it should be legally available in Ireland and what motivates those who argue for or against its availability.

Elective abortion, also known as therapeutic abortion, is the termination of a pregnancy before the foetus has grown to full term or is sufficiently developed to survive independently outside the womb. This should not be confused with the term spontaneous abortion, which refers to miscarriage. Regardless of the reasons for the termination there are still the issues of bereavement and loss around an abortion.

Abortion has been used in various cultures over the millennia as a means of population control. It is certain that abortion has been a feature, although not widely documented, of Irish society since earliest times. It was always possible, if one asked questions of those 'in the know' and had sufficient resources, to procure an abortion. However to do so is prohibited by section 58 of the Offences Against the Person Act, 1861. The actual offence is the procurement of a miscarriage and although the law was passed in the nineteenth century, it is still on the statute books today. Both men and women can be convicted under this legislation.

The decision to have an abortion is, according to author Denise Winn in her book *Experiences of Abortion*: 'rarely instant, automatic or pain-free'. The emotional consequences, as well as the physical effects of abortion, can be lifelong. Winn goes on to say: 'Abortion carries emotional connotations, to do with life and death, with fertility and womanhood, sexuality and identity.' For some women, abortion prevents them from ever bearing a child in the future.

The most recently available statistics on Irish women who have had abortions indicates that a substantial number of pregnancies, as many as one in ten, now end in abortion. In 1998 at least 5,300 women with Irish addresses had abortions in the UK. The majority of Irishwomen choosing abortion are unmarried and in their early to mid-twenties.

Abortion and emotions

Statistics about abortion always hide stark realities. Feelings of fear, anxiety, guilt, shock, panic, shame, sadness, relief, confusion, regret, loss, and bereavement, among other emotions, will inevitably accompany a woman's decision to have an abortion. Quoted in *Experiences of Abortion*, one psychotherapist/counsellor observes: 'Abortion is, literally, a loss and how people handle loss is personal to them . . . and the decision of individual women is as unique to them as the feelings and emotions which go with that decision.'

In a recent, detailed exploration of the issue of abortion, *Swimming Against The Tide — Feminist dissent on the issue of abortion,* edited by Angela Kennedy, it is argued that pre-abortion counselling, no matter how sensitive, cannot prepare a woman for how she may feel during and after the event. For this reason, expert post-abortion counselling would seem to be appropriate, although the need for this may only be recognised years after the event. Suppressed emotions often surface under a different guise and bereavement is a feature of the vast majority of abortions, because abortion involves death.

Counselling agencies can provide support for those faced with a crisis pregnancy and post-abortion counselling is available through some agencies. Anyone considering counselling of this nature ought to consider carefully the credentials and qualifications of those offering such services.

CHAPTER 7

Murder most foul

How safe are we?

When reports of yet another horrific murder hit the headlines it is tempting to assume that Ireland is a very unsafe place to live. Yet a close look at the available records reveals that the annual rate of homicide in the Republic of Ireland between 1972 and 1991 was less than ten per million per annum. In 1996, however, the number of violent deaths was forty-two and there has been a small increase in the number of murders committed in recent years. These statistics, of course, are little or no consolation to families who have been bereaved by the violent death of a family member.

Studies on homicide

The most recent study, *Homicide in Ireland,* was completed in 1995 by Dr Enda Dooley, Director of Prison Medical Services at the Department of Justice. While Dr Dooley does not consider his report a fully comprehensive review, it is quite a wide-ranging document, referring to a variety of homicides including murder, manslaughter, infanticide and psychiatric cases (where the defendant was unfit to plead or where murders were committed by the insane).

It seems that the majority of murder victims in

Ireland have been male. Most were aged between twenty and thirty-nine years of age and they died as a result of a blow or blows from a sharp instrument, a stabbing or assault. These deaths occurred either at home or in a public place and the perpetrator was usually male. In the case of sexual assaults, however, the majority of victims have been female and they died as a result of being strangled or asphyxiated. Again, the perpetrators were male.

The study also showed that nearly four out of every ten murderous assaults were planned, although the fatal outcome was not always intended. At least half of all murderers knew their victims. In a substantial number of murder cases either the victim or the murderer or both had consumed alcohol. Almost half the murders committed were impulsive and unplanned actions involving anger or rage. Fifteen percent of murders occurred during the commission of another crime. Only one case out of six hundred and ten investigated in Dr Dooley's study involved murder for financial gain. Nearly sixty percent of all assailants admitted their involvement in the death. (The report does not include murders committed by terrorists.)

It must be said that not all those who commit murder are tried for their crime. Every year a certain number of murders will not be solved and unfortunately, the longer a murder remains unsolved the less likely that it will be. In order for a person to be convicted of murder they have to be at least seven years old and be legally sane. The death must have been of a living person (not an unborn child) during peacetime. (Different criteria apply during wartime.) It must be proven that there was an intention to kill or cause serious injury to the deceased. Certain defences can be used in mitigation. If the accused person was acting in self-defence or the death was accidental or by misadventure, then the homicide may be considered excusable.

In the *Homicide in Ireland* study, one third of cases were 'nolle prosequi', where the case was not proceeded with. It is important to state that these cases were not acquittals, but that for various reasons it was not considered appropriate to try the case. Of those convicted of murder, fewer than fifty percent received a life sentence or a discretionary sentence.

In the case of aggravated murder (formerly capital murder) — the murder of an on-duty Garda or prison officer, or of a member of the government or of a foreign head of state or diplomat — there is a mandatory forty-year sentence. Attempted murder in these cases brings a mandatory twenty-year sentence.

Life sentences are generally fourteen years, but discretionary sentences can vary and, depending on the circumstances surrounding the murder, the convicted person could even get probation. Overly harsh or lenient sentences are usually appealed. Success rates in changing the initial verdict are also variable.

Emotions and the media

Emotions can run high during a murder trial and in the days following the conviction and sentencing of the perpetrator. Public outrage is often heightened by the age of the victim and the circumstances surrounding the killing. Family, friends and colleagues of murder victims may call for the death penalty. This is generally asked for in the heat of the moment, and usually in time, the desire for retribution becomes more important than the desire for revenge. Although the last execution in the Republic of Ireland took place in 1954 it wasn't until 1990 that the death penalty for capital offences was abolished.

Murder trials always generate great media interest. They make good copy and the tabloid nature of much of our current press coverage is such that some journalists will go to considerable lengths to get quotes from relatives, friends or neighbours. Even the most tenuous links are given importance and often the truth is sacrificed in the interests of a good story. Such media coverage is intrusive, unnecessary and ultimately unhelpful.

Death Sentence

A death sentence or sentence of execution (lawful homicide) may only be passed by a proper court when the accused has been lawfully convicted by that court. In 1964 the Criminal Justice Act revoked capital punishment for all crimes except treason and aggravated murder. The last people to receive the death sentence in the Republic of Ireland were Noel and Marie Murray, who were convicted in the mid-1970s for the capital murder of Garda Fallon. Since 1954 the practice in Ireland has been for death sentences to be commuted to life imprisonment. Their death sentence was commuted to life imprisonment. The last judicial execution in Ireland was that of Michael Manning. It took place in Mountjoy jail in April 1954. Manning was a twenty-five year old from Limerick. He was hanged after being condemned to death for the murder of a nurse.

A number of well-documented miscarriages of justice in the recent past clearly indicate that the execution of convicted murderers is not in society's best interest. In every part of the world where execution is retained as the ultimate legal sanction for murder, there are innocent people who die at the hands of the state.

Inevitably, the family of both murderer and victim suffer because of public perception, often fuelled by the interest of the media. The shame and sorrow suffered by the family of the perpetrator is often just as acute as that of the victim's family. The family of the victim will inevitably have the support of the general public, whereas there may be a tendency to apportion blame to the family of the convicted; there may be a sense that somehow other family members must be guilty by association. Counselling may be of benefit, but recovering self-esteem must, inevitably, take a long time.

CHAPTER 8

Suicide – self killing

Attitudes to suicide

Up to a few years ago suicide and attempted suicide were deemed to be criminal acts, a source of deep shame for the families and a cause of disdain towards the victims. In a religious sense they were considered to be mortally sinful. Victims of suicide were refused the rites of the Church and were not allowed burial in consecrated ground. The bodies of suicide victims were often treated with great indignity.

Enlightened thinking in recent times, however, has changed both the civil and religious status of suicides and attempted suicides, which are now viewed in psychological terms rather than in moral or legal terms. In 1993 the Criminal Law (Suicide) Act was introduced, effectively de-criminalising suicide and attempted suicide. However, encouraging a person to commit suicide or aiding and abetting a suicide are still considered to be serious crimes.

Prior to the enactment of the 1993 Act, suicides could not be recorded because the coroner's court in Ireland does not have the power to find that a crime has been committed. Under Irish law the coroner's inquest is only required to establish the cause of death; not to apportion blame.

Death wish

Many of us know people who engage in risky, life threatening behaviour. Whether they dabble in drugs, drive recklessly or partake in dangerous sports, we know that there is always a chance that they will 'come a cropper!' They know it too and Sigmund Freud had a theory relating to this kind of behaviour. He called it the death instinct or thanatos. These days it is commonly called a death wish. The person engaging in the activity may not have consciously thought their actions through. Then again maybe they have, and go ahead and do it anyway. Wish-fulfilment suicide is very common, although the coroner's verdict will not record it as such unless the evidence shows, beyond a reasonable doubt, that there was a suicidal intention on the part of the deceased.

Currently in Ireland, many more families and friends have had to face the trauma associated with suicide than ever before. In a survey of inquests within the area covered by the Office of the Dublin City Coroner, there were actually more deaths due to suicide than to road accidents between January and July of 1998. Thirteen of the fifty-four suicides were women. These sad statistics show that the ratio of male suicides to female suicides was more than four to one.

In Ireland, and throughout Europe, suicide is considered to have reached epidemic proportions. Apparently, suicide is the second biggest killer of young men in western society after road accidents.

Precisely why there has been such an increase in the number of recorded suicides is unclear. Those who have studied the phenomenon believe it may stem from the pressures of modern life, a lack of spiritual identity or a sense of rootlessness. Some have suggested that the number of self-inflicted deaths has not increased significantly at all, but that methods of recording them have improved. In addition there may have been a tendency in the past to cover up the actual cause of death because of the religious and social sanctions which might have applied if suicide were the stated cause of death.

In spite of a lessening of the stigma attached to suicide, there is still enormous embarrassment for the bereaved families. The 'not knowing' is immensely painful and even many years after the event, those left behind can suffer considerable guilt that somehow they might have done or said something to prevent their loved one from killing himself or herself.

Suicide notes

In *Voices of Death*, by Edwin Shreiden, the author deals with the issue of notes left by suicides: ' . . . if one could write a meaningful note, one would not have to commit suicide . . .' This would be especially true in the case of those who commit suicide out of anger or revenge, although a significant number of suicide notes studied in Ireland indicate that the victim was suffering from depression, which may be classed as a form of mental illness.

In his moving account of his life and ministry, *Dancing With Life*, Fr Vincent Travers OP, former parish priest of Tallaght, Dublin and chaplain to prisoners in Mountjoy Prison, devotes considerable space to the issue of suicide. Fr Travers writes that expert opinion on suicide suggests that the principal reason for it may be a sense among the victims that their problems will never end; that suicide seems the 'only way out'.

Copycat incidents are quite common and sometimes a spate of suicides can occur. The death of a famous personality, or even the break-up of a popgroup, can provoke unstable and impressionable people to get depressed to the point where they might be considering taking their own lives. There can be a sense among some that suicide is somehow romantic. This romantic notion is not new and was, perhaps, what the poet Wordsworth had in mind when he wrote that he was ' . . . half in love with easeful death'.

FACTS ON SUICIDE

- Many of those who intend to kill themselves tell someone of their intentions.
- Many suicidal people gamble with death and may still wish to live.
- Survivors of attempted suicide can find that thoughts about committing suicide come back, even though they may appear to be well again.
- Suicide occurs in all walks of life.
- It is often assumed that suicides result from mental illness, but less than 15% of those who take their own lives are clinically mentally ill. Most, it seems, are just deeply unhappy.

- Many people will think about suicide at some time in their life and it is a myth that those who talk about committing suicide don't do it.
- Significant factors in suicides are unemployment; alcohol and/or drug abuse; money problems; changes in family life; occupation.
- Men tend to use more dramatic methods of suicide than women such as hanging, shooting or drowning. They are also more likely to succeed in killing themselves.
- Women tend to use poisoning or self-mutilation as a means of suicide.

Sometimes people injure themselves deliberately but do not intend suicide. This is known as parasuicide. Often they do sufficient harm to themselves to cause death. Others intend to kill themselves and fail. Unlike other EU countries, it appears that equal numbers of Irish men and women are victims of parasuicide.

WHO IS MOST LIKELY TO COMMIT SUICIDE?

- Mainly men under the age of 25.
- Those over the age of 65.
- Those suffering from severe depression, hopelessness, alcoholism, drug addiction or gambling addiction.
- Those suffering from severe stress, whether sudden or continuous.
- Those who have made a suicide plan.
- Those with a history of attempted suicide or with a family history of suicide.
- Those who have a chronic debilitating illness.

- Those who have been diagnosed with a terminal illness.
- Those who have no communication skills.
- Those who have lost the love and esteem of a significant person or people in their lives.

The Report of the National Task Force on Suicide (1998) presents statistics which show that the suicide rate in Ireland is almost four and a half times the rate it was fifty years ago. The response of the Task Force to the virtual suicide epidemic in Ireland in recent times has been to make certain positive recommendations towards handling the issue very sensitively. The National Task Force on Suicide received a huge number of submissions, a substantial number of which were from coroners around the country.

Some of the main recommendations in the report were that:
- Garda training should include the issue of suicide awareness.
- In-service training in suicide awareness should be made available to serving Garda members.
- Mental health programmes for children should be part of the Social, Personal and Health Education (SPHE) programmes in both primary and post-primary schools.
- Guidelines should be provided for sensitive media reporting of suicides in order to reduce or prevent copy-cat incidents.

Counselling for the suicidal

Someone who is suicidal needs real friendship. Talking frankly about their suicidal feelings can be very helpful. Empty assurances from the listener such as 'I know how you feel' and criticism or advice such as 'What I would do if I was you' are not helpful. Silent company can prove more valuable than words. Suggest that the person who is in trouble talks to the **Samaritans** or to someone else who might be able to help.

Suicide research is ongoing and the National Association of Suicidology and the National Suicide Research Foundation continue to explore the phenomenon. The pioneering work carried out in the area of suicide by the late Dr Michael J Kelleher and the work of the many other dedicated professionals and volunteers must be acknowledged.

As a result of the work of these organisations a special report form is now supplied to the Garda, when deaths are being investigated, so that more accurate statistics than before about suicide will be available to the researchers.

For those left behind

Suicide elicits incalculable grief and anguish, anger, frustration and unanswered questions from the relatives and friends of the dead person. The adjustments which must be made emotionally and socially by those left behind are, perhaps, far greater than those which arise after any other form of death. Individual and family counselling is particularly advisable as many people who receive counselling find it very helpful. Relations, neighbours and friends can also be very supportive to the people bereaved. Parents, brothers, sisters and friends generally do all they can to love, support and encourage each other in time of crisis. What we don't know – and can never know – is why a person chooses to take his or her own life. This is the mystery that is suicide.

The coroner's role in suicide

According to Dr Bartley Sheehan, spokesperson for the Coroners' Association of Ireland, establishing uniformity of verdicts in the case of suicides is most important. He himself has recorded many suicide verdicts, yet he is aware that some coroners have not done so, considering that a suicide verdict might be challenged. A suicide verdict will only be given when it has been established 'beyond all reasonable doubt' that the person died as a result of that person's deliberate intention to kill himself or herself.

Cases of suicide are treated with the utmost sensitivity by the coroners. Bereaved families are extended great courtesy and the condolences of the court. The option is also given for those who might be upset by the details of the autopsy to leave the room while this evidence is heard; a most considerate and humane approach.

Missing persons

Around 1,500 people go missing in Ireland every year. Many of them turn up alive and well, while some are found to be suffering from depression. It must be said that if a person does not want to be found they can succeed in disappearing entirely.

Some, but not all, of those who disappear are the victims of suicide while others are murder victims. Recently publicised cases of disappearances show how distressed a family can become when someone they love goes missing. Family and friends suffer the agony of not knowing whether the person is dead or alive. In the case of a missing person who is dead there is some comfort in eventually finding a body to bury. The long searches which are carried out to retrieve the bodies of those lost at sea or in drowning accidents or otherwise are a clear indication of this basic need.

Legally a person must be missing for seven years before they can be declared dead. Insurance companies have different criteria for the settlement of claims in this regard. Some may expect the beneficiaries of the person's estate to wait until the legal requirement has been met, or they may make an interim ex-gratia payment with a full settlement after seven years. All reasonable efforts will have to be made to contact the missing person. Cases in which a fugitive from the law has disappeared are unlikely to be settled quickly. Presumably, if the missing person were to turn up alive, then any monies paid out would have to be returned.

CHAPTER 9

Euthanasia – easy death

Assisted suicide

The issue of assisted suicide has received a lot of media coverage recently. The highly publicised case of Dr Jack Kevorkian in the United States has generated a heated debate over whether or not it is ethical for a physician to deliberately kill a patient. Dr Kevorkian's defence in court has been that he only ever assisted the death of patients who had consciously and sanely expressed their wish to die. In spite of this he was recently convicted of second degree murder.

In the UK the renowned author and journalist Sir Ludovic Kennedy has championed the cause of those who support euthanasia. In Ireland this cause has been defended by Dr Paddy Leahy, an outspoken commentator, social campaigner and advocate of euthanasia. In a moving radio interview with broadcaster Vincent Browne, Dr Leahy provoked considerable discussion about the ethics and morality of euthanasia. He stated at the time that it was his intention to travel to Thailand to die with assistance, but he was refused entry. Dr Leahy subsequently returned to Ireland and died peacefully at home of natural causes. The legal position in most countries is that assisted suicide and euthanasia are not acceptable and in even the most liberal societies, those convicted of involvement will serve time for murder or attempted murder. No doubt the debate for and against euthanasia, which began in the UK and the US in the 1930s, will continue.

For those who would like to study the issue further, law lecturer Patrick Hanafin's excellent study, *Last Rights – death, dying and the law in Ireland*, is worth reading. Dr Hanafin observes how the institutions of medicine and law have shaped our perception of death and how far the law should impinge on individual autonomy. He suggests that a more patient-oriented approach should be taken by the law in the resolution of medical dilemmas. He eloquently argues the case for legislators to tackle the law in this area, thus avoiding the situation where the courts are required to adjudicate in complex matters of medical ethics regarding people's rights relating to death. This, of course, will demand great courage on the part of legislators and it may well be quite some time before it becomes a reality. Recent US Supreme Court decisions have re-affirmed the legal ban on physician–assisted suicide in that country.

Living wills
As a result of legal moves in other jurisdictions the idea of a 'living will' has come up for public discussion in Ireland. In a living will it is suggested that while a person is well, they might choose to establish clear guidelines for their treatment (or indeed lack of treatment) in the event of their becoming incapable of

speaking for themselves at a later stage. Many people believe that it is reasonable for a person to request that heroic treatment measures should not be employed to save their life if their quality of life were to become unbearable. In a recent High Court case in London, Annie Lindsel, a victim of motor-neurone disease argued for the right not to be treated against her will when her condition became acute. According to her leading counsel, Lord Lester of Herne QC, her case was an attempt to clarify the criminal law and good medical practice in relation to the palliative care of terminally-ill patients. As in Ireland, the law in the UK still remains unclear regarding the legal concepts of intention and causation.

NTBR directive

It is policy in Irish hospitals not to resuscitate patients who are dying when to do so would be unethical. This is not the same as euthanasia; rather it is a policy of allowing nature to take its course and is most humane. The Not To Be Resuscitated (NTBR) directive is only given in specific circumstances and is always applied within very strict medical, ethical and legal guidelines.

With the development of highly sophisticated medical techniques and wonder drugs, a person's life can be prolonged in ways that would never have been possible in previous generations. In some cases, the use of antibiotics can have the effect of prolonging a person's life beyond what might be considered reasonable.

In the past, pneumonia was known as the 'old people's friend', as it was often the cause of death. Even today, with the use of antibiotics, there will come a point when the body can no longer respond to medication and it is reasonable for medical staff to forego heroic efforts to keep the person alive just for the sake of doing so. It is important for us to consider whether or not we wish to keep the dying person alive for his or her own sake or for ours. One way or the other, death will have its day and we need to consider what action is in the best interests of the person who is dying.

Until the major issues of living wills, euthanasia and the right to die are more fully explored, we must encourage all those who have the responsibility of caring for the living and the dying to adhere to the highest moral, ethical and legal standards.

CHAPTER 10

When we die

The act of dying

Some people die in their sleep, thus experiencing a peaceful exit from this world. Others die instantaneously, or almost so, from stroke, heart attack or in an accident. The majority of people, however, die more slowly. Death is usually a process of gradual decline as the major organs cease to function and eventually the heart and breathing stop altogether.

There comes a time for the one who is dying to 'let go'. There is also a time when the living relatives and friends must let go too. In our understandable anxiety to avoid the agony of loss, we may hold on to our loved one, willing them to stay with us for a while longer.

It is quite common for a person who is dying to get an apparent burst of energy some time, perhaps a day or two, before their death. They may become lucid and cheerful and may acknowledge those present. This can be a source of false comfort to the family, who mistakenly believe that their loved one is recovering. In Irish this was commonly termed '*an biseach roimh báis*' which means the improvement before death.

There is no doubt that it can be very hard to watch another person make the transition from life to death. It is often profoundly disturbing to see a loved one die, particularly if they are struggling for breath or very clearly in pain. This is why palliative care, which is designed to give symptomatic relief rather than to provide a cure, can prove so useful to the sufferer and his or her family.

As death approaches

Professor Hinton wisely observed that: 'death has no timetable; there is no script to be followed and there is no control over what happens'. As death approaches, the extremities — fingers, toes, arms and legs — may become very cold. Breathing can become shallower and more laboured (called Cheyne–Stokes breathing). There can be a gurgling sound in the person's throat, which is often called the death rattle. As the last of the air is expelled from the lungs there may be a deep sigh. A number of spasms, called the death throes, may also occur throughout the whole body as the person dies. The eyes become glazed and the pupils become fixed and dilated. However, not everyone dies in this manner. Some people just slip away with hardly a sound or movement. No two deaths are exactly the same.

When has 'death' occured?

Modern medicine, and the law, states that death has occurred when all circulatory functions (movement of blood through the veins) and respiratory functions (breathing) cease irreversibly. Alternatively, the medical profession may use a definition of brain death where all functions of the entire brain (upper and lower) have ceased irreversibly. In this case, there are no visible or detectable signs of life and the person is incapable of any functions or communication. The upper brain, called the cerebrum, is responsible for all our thoughts and feelings and our conscious behaviour. The lower brain, called the brain stem, is responsible for reflex actions like yawning and breathing and sleeping.

When a person is dead they cannot think or experience emotion. The person is said to be brain dead and cannot feel pain and they never regain consciousness. This is not the same as persistent vegetative state (PVS) where the person remains unconscious but still has the capacity to breathe, either independently or with the aid of a respirator.

The body after death

Soon after death the deceased person's body cools down. This is because the body's natural process of combusting food to generate body heat is no longer functioning. The cooling down is called algor mortis. The level of body cooling can sometimes be used by a pathologist to ascertain the time of death.

Between five and ten hours after death the body stiffens. This is called rigor mortis and is caused by the coagulation of muscle proteins. The process lasts for three or four days and is significantly reduced by the embalming process. As the blood settles in the body the underside of the body may take on a reddish, blue discolouration known as livor mortis.

In the past, before rigor mortis had set in, a cloth or bandage would be tied like a headscarf under the dead person's chin. This was to keep the lower jaw from sagging, causing the mouth to remain open. This is rarely done nowadays. Instead, a pillow is placed on the person's chest and under the chin. It does the same job, keeping the mouth completely closed, but in a much less dramatic fashion.

The skin of the eyelids is extremely thin and soon after death contraction of the eyelids can cause them to spring open again. Hence the ancient practice of placing coins on the eyes to keep them shut. Nowadays, a small pad of cotton wool is placed under the eyelids, keeping them perfectly closed and natural looking as though the person were asleep. It is standard practice in hospitals and nursing homes to wash the body of the dead person. This is done as a mark of respect and for hygienic reasons. As there may be seepage from body openings, suitable stanchings are applied and bowel gases are released.

Preparing the dead body
The vast majority of people who die in Ireland are embalmed. This is not the detailed process carried out by the ancient Egyptians. It is done mainly for cosmetic reasons, so that the family and friends of the deceased can view the body without being unduly upset. The embalmer has been trained to handle the dead body with great respect. The voluntary code of ethics of embalmers (also known as morticians) and funeral directors dictates that the body should be prepared for viewing by the family in such a way that the deceased is as presentable as possible. The sight of a dead body, which is prepared so that the person almost looks as if

they were asleep, is much more bearable and acceptable than the sight of one which has not been well prepared.

The embalmer safely disposes of the person's blood while replacing it with a preservative fluid called formaldehyde, which has a small amount of pink dye added. The amount of fluid required depends on the age, sex, weight and size of the person. The gums are stitched together and the eyes are firmly closed. For obvious health and safety reasons, those who die of AIDS or drug abuse or who have had hepatitis cannot be embalmed. Embalming may involve the removal of internal organs (the viscera) but this is not generally the case. The dead person's hair may be washed and then combed or brushed in the way they would have worn it in life. Some embalmers may ask for a photograph of the deceased for this purpose. Cosmetics are sometimes used on the deceased. It is important to state that the next of kin may choose not to have their deceased relative embalmed.

The older practice of burying people in a shroud (rather like a religious habit) is no longer as common as it used to be. The majority of people are now buried in their own clothes. Heart pacemakers and any metal plates in the body must be removed by the embalmer if the deceased is to be cremated. This is for safety reasons associated with the cremation process.

After-death examination

Doctors are in the business of saving lives, but death is a fact which cannot be denied and since earliest times, those involved in practising the art of medicine have needed to study human anatomy. Doctors can learn a huge amount from the examination of dead bodies. An after-death examination (autopsy or postmortem) can provide useful information about the cause of death and about the effects of illness on the human body.

Medical staff in hospitals may request permission of the family or next of kin to hold an autopsy. The family may or may not agree to this. If, however, a medico-legal autopsy has been ordered by a coroner, then the family or next of kin cannot refuse. If the cause of death is known, then a postmortem is not always necessary.

If the death is sudden or unexpected or because of suicide, accident or violence, then the district coroner must be notified. The coroner will then arrange for a postmortem to be carried out. This will usually be performed by a hospital pathologist or, in some cases, by the state pathologist or the deputy state pathologist.

Should an autopsy show that the person died of natural causes, it will not be necessary to inquire into the death any further; no inquest will be held and a coroner's certificate regarding the cause of death can be issued. It is important to state that the body of the deceased is not disfigured during a postmortem. The family and friends of the deceased can view the body afterwards, as though no autopsy had taken place.

CHAPTER 11

The coroner and the law

The role of the coroner

Many people have heard of the coroner but do not fully understand the functions of the coroner at the coroner's court. Television programmes, especially those from the US give the impression that the coroner is a kind of detective whose job it is to solve murder mysteries. The law relating to the coroner in Ireland is not the same as in other countries.

The title 'coroner' or 'crowner' in the past indicated that the appointed person was a representative of the crowned monarch. The role of the coroner was first mentioned in England in 1194, while the earliest known reference to the coroner in Ireland is 1215. There is some evidence that the office of coroner may have existed in Ireland since 1212. The city archivist office in Dublin Corporation maintains a list of coroners for Dublin City from 1215.

The coroner's remit involved finding out the cause of sudden deaths. The coroner could impound any instrument, sword or knife for example (known as the deodand) which caused the death. In later years, when a person could be killed by a coach or steam engine, for example, confiscating the deodand became impractical. The coroner could also impound any treasure–trove discovered in his district. Although this role is still mentioned in the Coroner's Act 1962, in practice it no longer falls to the coroner to deal with such finds. In Northern Ireland the coroner can and still does deal with treasure–trove. In June 1997 Mr Roger McLernon, Her Majesty's Coroner for the East Tyrone and Magharafelt District judged that Bronze Age Gold artefacts found in Cookstown in 1995 were treasure–trove and the property of the Crown. The UK Coroner's Act was amended in 1988 and in general coroners throughout Ireland follow similar procedures.

Coroners in Ireland

At present there are forty-nine coroners in the Republic of Ireland. Each coroner is appointed to a district by a local authority, under the auspices of the Minister for Justice. Currently a coroner must be either a qualified barrister or solicitor, or a qualified medical practitioner. Many are doubly qualified.

The office of the coroner is independent, with responsibility for investigating the medical and legal aspects of certain deaths. The coroner's job is to establish whether a reported death was from natural causes or from unnatural causes. If the death was from unnatural causes, then an inquest is required by law.

When a death is sudden, violent or unnatural then quite a number of people have a legal responsibility to notify the death to the coroner. Alternatively the death may be reported to a Garda sergeant or to a higher ranking Garda officer. Doctors, registrars, funeral directors, householders and those in charge of premises where the death occurred are so obliged, but in common law any person may notify the coroner about a death.

DEATHS WHICH MUST BE REPORTED TO THE CORONER

- The death of a person at home or at another residence, where the person is not attended by a doctor during the final illness or within a month of the date of death.
- A death which is sudden, unexpected, of an unknown cause or as a result of accident, suicide or murder.
- Certain deaths in hospitals and all deaths of prisoners.
- Certain stillbirths, all sudden infant deaths or the death of a child in care.

When a death is reported, a Garda officer can act as an officer of the coroner, assisting in the formal identification of the deceased. It is important for relatives not to be alarmed if a Garda officer takes a statement about the circumstances of the death. This does not imply that the death is suspicious.

Funeral arrangements or arrangements for organ donation cannot be made without the permission of the coroner if the coroner's office is involved already in the death. The coroner will indicate when the body will be available for burial, and cremation cannot take place without an appropriate certificate from the coroner.

What is an inquest?
In Ireland an inquest is a public inquiry. It is inquisitorial and not adversarial. The coroner, working

with or without a jury, will enquire into the circumstances of a particular death and neither civil nor criminal liability will be investigated or even considered. It is the function of the inquest to establish the facts, i.e. the identity of the person who has died and how, when, where and in what circumstances they died. These facts are then recorded as a matter of public record and are available also to the Registrar of Deaths. Verdicts handed down in a coroner's court range from an open verdict where the cause of the death remains unclear, accidental death, misadventure, suicide or unlawful killing (in certain circumstances).

No person can be censured or exhonorated in an inquest. If criminal proceedings or investigations are ongoing, then the coroner will adjourn the inquest until these are completed and the inquest is put down for mention at a later date, usually about three months.

In November 1997 the Supreme Court made a number of pronouncements relating to the public policy underlying a coroner's inquest. Among other things, the Supreme Court identified the need to provide appropriate investigations by duly qualified personnel (coroners) into certain deaths. It also identified the duties of the coroner, in the public's interest, to establish the medical cause of death; to allay suspicion or rumour, to draw attention to matters of public safety (which if unremedied could lead to further deaths); to advance medical knowledge and also to preserve the legal interests of the family (and heirs) of the deceased and those of other interested parties.

When a doctor has given a medical report under

oath, during an inquest, the coroner will then take the doctor through the evidence. He will ask questions, clarifying all matters of evidence and the doctor is expected to try to explain the medical terminology, especially if it is a jury inquest. The coroner decides who will be called as a witness and evidence is provided in a logical sequence.

Witnesses at an inquest will have provided a written statement of evidence in advance. This is called a deposition and as part of the procedure of the inquest, the depositions will be read in open court either by the witnesses themselves or by the clerk of the court. All witnesses are required to swear an oath that their evidence is true.

The witnesses at an inquest may be questioned by any properly interested persons or by their legal representatives. The inquest is not a trial, however. It is an inquiry into the facts surrounding the circumstance of the death in question.

A JURY IS REQUIRED AT THE INQUEST IF:

- the death was due to murder, manslaughter or infanticide.
- the person died in prison.
- the death was due to an accident at work or due to occupational disease or poisoning or from a notifiable disease.
- the death was because of a road traffic accident or circumstances which unremedied could lead to further loss of life.

Inquest juries

Inquest juries are made up of ordinary citizens. Between six and twelve jurors are required, with an average of eight or nine. It is the jury and not the coroner who will give the verdict. If the jury at the inquest fails to agree on a verdict, a majority verdict must be accepted or, where a majority verdict cannot be reached, the coroner can discharge the jury and hold a new inquest.

If a jury inquest is adjourned, and only evidence of identification has been given, the inquest can be reconvened with a different jury.

Asking questions at an inquest

A person with a proper interest in an inquest may ask questions of a witness or a legal representitive may ask questions on the person's behalf. If the death occurred in hospital or in prison or in some other institution then a representative may ask questions. Anyone who was responsible for the death in some way may also ask questions, as may representatives of insurance companies.

Trade union representatives; the deceased person's employer; Health and Safety Authority inspectors or others (at the discretion of the coroner) may ask questions at an inquest if the death was as a result of an accident at work.

Occasionally inquests are reported in the media and every effort is made to treat inquests with the greatest sensitivity. Bereaved families are given every consideration, including the option to leave the court while the autopsy report is being given.

Interim death certificate

If the cause of death has not been established before the inquest, the coroner can provide an interim death certificate. While this is not a legally binding document it will generally be accepted by banks and building societies so that the deceased person's affairs can be settled. The staff at the coroners' offices are both sympathetic and helpful. Much credit is due to them as they carry out a difficult job with great sensitivity and courtesy.

CHAPTER 12

Donating one's body to science

No greater love

According to Christian tradition a person can have 'no greater love' than to lay down his or her life for a friend. Some surpass this maxim by donating their mortal remains for the furtherance of medical science. The departments of anatomy of the nation's medical schools are always grateful to people who make such a generous bequest. Here no taboo exists around death. Dealing with human anatomy is a necessary element of the education of future medical professionals such as doctors, dentists, nurses and physiotherapists.

The Anatomy Act

The Anatomy Act was passed in 1832. While the government of the day recognised the need for human bodies for legitimate medical purposes in Great Britain and Ireland, appropriate regulations were required. An inspectorate was set up to ensure that all bodies acquired by medical schools had a death certificate and that the deceased or their next of kin had given their permission. Provision was also made in the act for the suitable burial of the person's remains afterwards.

The Anatomy Act of 1832 still applies in the Republic of Ireland. In Northern Ireland the Anatomy (Northern

Ireland) Order 1992 applies. Bodies are donated by means of a bequest. A person who wishes to leave his or her body for anatomical study can do so in writing, giving an expression of intent. The various medical schools in the country each require up to thirty bodies every year. If, when a person dies, the next of kin do not wish to donate their loved one's body, they are not legally bound to do so.

Two identical forms are supplied, one to be sent to the medical school and the other to be kept with the person's will or other personal papers. When a person dies there can be no guarantee that their body will be accepted. In fact, if any organs, other than the eyes have been removed for transplantation then the body cannot be received for donation. Acceptance is also denied if a post mortem has been carried out on the body.

A designated funeral director will deal with transferring the remains to the medical school and the cost of removal is met by the school in question. If the family chooses to hold a service for the deceased with the person's remains present, ideally this should take place within 48 hours of the death. Some families choose to hold a memorial service without the remains present.

Bodies which have been donated are preserved using a combination of formaldehyde, phenol, alcohol and fungicide. The preservation process is different from the embalming carried out by funeral directors. Bodies may be kept for up to three years and with the permission of the relatives, the body may be kept for a fourth year in some medical schools.

Funeral arrangements

When all studies on the body are complete the family or executor of the deceased are duly notified that the body is no longer needed and that a date has been set for the funeral, to be paid for by the school. Because of the high cost of burial nowadays, families are asked to consider cremation of the remains. Families who choose to attend the final committal ceremony may have the deceased buried in the medical school's plot. If cremation is the chosen option the ashes may be scattered as the relatives wish. Alternatively, the family may choose to meet the cost of private burial arrangements, although the medical school will usually provide a coffin and cover the costs of removal to the cemetery.

The magnanimous gesture made by those who leave their remains for scientific study advances the training of medical students and the improvement of surgical techniques. It also furthers medical and surgical research. The colleges of anatomy recognise the valuable contribution made by those generous people who bequeath their bodies. Annual memorial services are held by some of the medical schools to honour those who have bequeathed their remains.

CHAPTER 13

Arranging a funeral

Why have a funeral?

There is a deep psychological value in holding a funeral service for a dead loved one. It helps all those involved to come to terms with the reality and finality of death. There is a sense of completion when the person's body is buried or when their ashes are interred or scattered.

There are very few individuals or families nowadays who choose to arrange a funeral without the assistance of a funeral director. It can be done without professional assistance, but it is inevitably difficult and trying, although not impossible. A useful resource for further information is the *New Natural Death Handbook* (1997).

Thinking ahead

Although we all know we must die sometime, few of us are prepared to make arrangements in advance. If a loved one is dying, those close by will rarely choose to make arrangements regarding the funeral until the person has actually died.

When a family first make contact with a funeral director's office, it is generally after a death has occurred. This is surprising, as the vast proportion of deaths are expected and the family will usually have had some time to come to terms with the impending death of a loved one. The person the family are making arrangements for will, more than likely, be in hospital, in a nursing home or in a hospice.

It would make sense, therefore, for some members of the family to start making enquiries about funeral arrangements *before* the actual death occurs. Some people, however, have the feeling that this is morbid and that it may in some way hasten the death of their loved one. Consequently they will postpone making arrangements until the very last moment.

Choosing a funeral director

The vast majority of families, it seems, tend to approach a specific funeral director on the basis of some knowledge of the work of that person or on the proximity of the funeral home. Whatever the reason for choosing a certain funeral director, there are things which the bereaved and the public in general should consider.

Funeral directors are service providers and consumers have the same rights regarding these services as they have regarding any other service. As with any other person's services you employ, payment is required. When an individual or family approaches a funeral director, however, they are usually in a state of emotional distress. For this reason it important to be aware that one can easily go over the top in making choices regarding the services required and end up incurring unnecessary expenses.

Payment options

Any services provided by a funeral undertaker must be paid for in full. Payment is expected reasonably promptly, in advance in some cases, as the outlay by the funeral company may be considerable. The undertakers may be prepared to wait a week or two, but greater delays will have to be agreed in advance.

There are several options available to people when arranging funeral expenses in advance. Older people tend to have small insurance policies which will yield about £2,000 or £3,000. Not all policies will yield as much as this and it is often quite a shock for families to find that a policy which had been paid over decades will only realise £100 or £200, if even that.

If the deceased has no insurance policy, then it will fall to the family or executor to pay the funeral bill and recoup the money later from the dead person's estate, if there is one. State assistance towards funeral expenses is available if family circumstances warrant it. Applications for assistance can be made through the local social welfare office.

THINGS TO THINK ABOUT

- Don't make all the arrangements on your own. If possible, bring one or two family members with you. Apart from the possibility of being over-zealous in incurring expenses if you are alone, there can be disagreement over the arrangements. In the high emotion of bereavement tempers can flare and some members of the family can feel left out. While it is impossible to keep everyone happy with every choice, the support of others is a safety net.

- Consider a reasonable budget and take into account what you know of the deceased. Would they have been satisified with an elaborate, expensive funeral or would a modest arrangement be more appropriate? There is no disrespect in shopping around!

- The funeral director will need information about the death, i.e. who died; when, where and how the death occurred; the age, occupation and religion of the deceased. The height and the build of the deceased will be required, as will the name of the doctor or other authorised person who certified the death. Details for the name plate inscription on the coffin will also be needed.

- The cost of coffins can vary substantially and it makes little sense, for example, to purchase an elaborate casket when cremation has been chosen rather than burial.

- Some families have a plot in a particular cemetery and, depending on circumstances, a previously used grave may be re-used. Different cemeteries will have differing arrangements about the advance purchase of graves. Some people choose to purchase a double plot when they are buying a grave so that the plot will, in effect, hold four or more coffins. Permission may be required of the grave owner for the use of the plot.

- If cremation is the chosen option, then decisions regarding disposal of the ashes will have to be made.

The ashes might be placed in the columbarium wall in the cemetery or placed in the cemetery garden or disposed of privately, in which case an urn will be required.

- Choices regarding embalming must also be made. It must be emphasised that embalming is not obligatory. Hygenic treatment of the body is an alternative. Either way, preparation and laying out of the body will be necessary.

- The family will have to choose how the deceased should be dressed. Many choose to use the person's own clothes or alternatively they might decide on a mortuary robe, habit or shroud.

- If the body of the deceased is to be put on view, then decisions about bringing the body home or using a funeral parlour must be made. Additional costs may be incurred either for the additional removal to the person's home or for the use of the funeral home.

- While it has been customary for families to place the deceased's body on view, this may not be appropriate if the person was disfigured – as in a road traffic accident or a fire or through serious illness.

- Funeral directors make a charge for arranging a funeral, for out-of-hours arrangements, for calling out to the family home and for making disbursements on behalf of the client.

- Disbursements consist of the purchase and opening of the grave, newspaper announcements, flowers, church offerings and gratuities, crematorium and cremation fees, doctor's fees and payments to church organist and/or singers.

- Costs for the hearse and funeral car(s) will be incurred for the removal, for the burial itself and any additional removals. The number of bearers will affect the overall cost.
- If a religious service is required, undertakers may act on behalf of the family, but the personal touch can make a big difference. Local clergy are always anxious to assist bereaved families in making the funeral service as personal and memorable as possible. They will discuss Scripture readings and music appropriate to the liturgy and ask details about the deceased and the bereaved family and friends in order to make mention of them during the ceremony.
- Newspapers, some local radio stations and the Internet carry death notices on a daily basis giving details of the date and place of a person's death and informing friends and relatives of the deceased of the times for the removal and the funeral. However, giving an exact address from which the funeral will take place is not advisable. Sadly, there are those who might use such information to target the empty house for burglary. Most bereaved families take the precaution of asking a neighbour to 'house-sit' while the funeral is taking place.
- Undertakers can also arrange for a death grant application and can usually make the necessary forms available. They cannot be expected, however, to make representations to the Department of Social, Community and Family Affairs on behalf of families.
- The final payment for the funeral is, for most

families, a debt of honour. By paying the funeral director's fees there is a sense of completion; a sense that all that could be done for the deceased has been done.

AFTERWARDS

- Some families choose to wait a while before arranging for a headstone to be erected over the deceased person's grave. Currently the costs for placing a monument can range from just under one thousand pounds to several thousand pounds.
- Traditionally, many Irish families purchase *In Memoriam* cards or bookmarks in order to commemorate their deceased loved ones. These may consist of a photograph and details of the deceased along with a prayer or a poem or words of wisdom. The costs vary according to the number and style of items chosen. Dedicated printing houses also sell printed *Appreciation Cards*. Prices for these vary also.
- Local and national newspapers often carry anniversary notices for deceased people. For some, these very personal tributes have a particular function in the grieving process and, many years after the person's death, can provide comfort and solace and a public recognition that the pain of loss may have eased but not ended. Ultimately, individuals and families must make their own choices regarding these notices.

CHAPTER 14

The funeral service

Funeral customs

In spite of the fact that fewer Irish people regularly attend church, the vast majority of funerals in this country involve leaving the person's remains in church overnight and having a funeral Mass or Service the following morning, with the burial or cremation afterwards.

There are different customs associated with funerals in different parts of the country too. Although the practice of 'waking' the dead overnight has fallen into disuse, a growing number of families are taking their loved ones back to the family home even for a few hours before removal to the church. In some parts of the country the funeral takes place over three days rather than two.

Death and philosophy

The realisation that we must all die is the stuff of philosophy. Socrates said that: 'the true philosopher makes death and dying their profession.' While Western philosophy is not entirely bound up with religious and theological thinking, the philosophy of the East is very much a part of the religious and cultural framework from which it sprang.

In the last few decades many Westerners have looked to other spiritual philosophies for direction and comfort. Although Ireland has been labelled as a post-Christian society, there are still some very important elements of the practice of the Christian religion which remain deeply rooted in our culture. Not least of these is the rite of Christian burial.

The vast majority of Irish people, regardless of how often or seldom they visited the church in their lifetime, desire 'a decent Christian burial', and regardless of what anyone might think or say, they are entitled to the last rites of their Church.

The ceremonies around death are as important today as they were in Neolithic times. We have a deep rooted need to acknowledge the life and death of those whom we love. It has been said that the funeral rite is far less for the dead than it is for those who are still alive and 'left behind'. Even the phrase 'left behind' is of significance. It speaks to us of a life after death, that the dead person has 'gone before us' and that they have indeed 'gone to a better place'.

Signs of mourning

Until the late 1960s those who were grieving a death showed publicly that they were in mourning. The wearing of black clothes or a black tie or arm-band or a black diamond on a coat sleeve was a clear indication that someone close had died. After a month, or so, the mourning clothes were put aside, and those around acknowledged that you were resuming a 'normal life'. That was not to suggest that you had completely recovered from your loss but rather that you had reached a certain point in the grieving process. One wonders why this public display of mourning fell into disuse. Was it due, perhaps, to a growing sense of unease and discomfort within Irish society with public expressions of grief? Was it part of the growing taboo about death?

'*Ná déan nós agus ná bris nós* . . . Don't make a tradition and don't break a tradition.' So the old Irish saying goes. So it is that the vast majority of Irish people who die are buried with great ceremony in their local cemetery. The family plot can hold great significance and without the traditional tombstone, many of those tracing their family roots would lose the trail.

Choosing a coffin

Choosing a coffin for a loved one can hold great significance. There has been a tendency, in recent times, for families to choose more and more elaborate coffins, moving away from the traditional wooden box to coffins such as the American lead-lined casket. It is significant that the choice doesn't matter at all to the one who is dead. For those who wish to be environmentally friendly, there is an option to use a cardboard coffin. Currently, Irish law does not allow for the use of a body-bag or shroud only. The stipulation is that a coffin should be made of wood or wood product. So-called woodland burials are unavailable in Ireland, as yet. A woodland burial consists of burying the body in a shroud or cardboard coffin in a designated woodland area with a tree planted on the gravesite.

Nowadays coffins are lined with satin-like material and the final task of the funeral undertaker before the coffin is closed, is to cover the face of the deceased with the cloth. The lid is usually screwed into place rather than being nailed, a sound which many relatives might find hard to bear.

Organising the plot

It is possible to purchase a specific plot in some cemeteries, although in others, you can only pay for the right to be buried in that cemetery. The location of your grave will depend on when you die. Municipal cemeteries tend to be quite well organised nowadays and pathways are provided to allow visitors easy access to graves.

The method of transporting the body to and from the church and subsequently to the cemetery or crematorium can be of very great significance too. In some parts of the country, the back of the hearse is left open and the mourners walk in procession behind. In other areas the coffin is carried in stages by family and friends. It is usually, though not always, the male relatives and friends who act as pall bearers. The lowering of the coffin into the grave differs from one area to another also. In some cemeteries the gravediggers let the coffin down. Sometimes the family does it.

Horse-drawn hearses used to be the order of the day before sleek motorised ones became available. Some funeral undertakers can still provide a horse-drawn service if that is what the family requires, provided the distance is not too great. The cost is not as expensive as one might assume.

Cremation

We know from archaeological evidence that the ancient Irish cremated their dead. They then placed the remains in elaborate urns and entombed them along with grave goods – items they believed could be used by the deceased in the afterlife. With the coming of Christianity, however, cremation was discontinued. It was deemed a pagan practice, destroying the work of God's creation and preventing the resurrection of the body on the last day.

It was not until 1963 that the code of Canon Law in the Catholic Church lifted the ban on cremation for Catholics, although the practice was not encouraged. Today, however, cremation is much more common among all Christian denominations with the rising costs of burials and the shortage of available land for cemeteries.

Glasnevin Cemetery will now no longer have the only crematorium in Dublin, following the construction of two further crematoria in Mount Jerome Cemetery and Shanganagh Cemetery. There is also a crematorium in Belfast. The new facilities in Mt. Jerome and Shanganagh will alleviate the pressure as cremation increases in popularity. The Irish fear of or distaste for cremation has diminished, although the number of cremations in comparison to interrments is still rather low. However, as funeral costs continue to rise and as land for burial becomes increasingly scarce, cremation seems to be a more viable option. The Mt. Jerome and Shanganagh crematoria, unlike their counterpart in Glasnevin, will be capable of dealing with cardboard coffins as well as the standard wooden coffin.

When cremation has been chosen, there is a short commital service similar to the one at a graveside before the coffin is removed from view. The coffin does not go directly into the cremation machine. It is stored by the staff of the crematorium until they are ready to complete the process, in fact it may be several hours before the body is put into the furnace. Special furnaces reduce the body and coffin to a residue which is further reduced to a fine ash. The ashes are then collected and placed in a wooden, metal or ceramic container and returned to the family within a few days.

Removal of the ashes
After the cremation the relatives can choose to dispose of the ashes in their own way. Some people bury the ashes in a family plot. Others choose to place the ashes in a memorial wall, known as a columbarium. They can then place a small plaque on the wall commemorating their loved one. There is only one columbarium in Ireland and it is in Glasnevin Cemetery. Some families choose to scatter the ashes of the deceased in the Glasnevin Garden of Remembrance or at some other personal and often significant location as appropriate.

If a person's remains are sent to Dublin for cremation, the ashes are returned to the funeral director, who will then inform the family that the ashes are available for collection and disposal. Occasionally families simply can't bear to complete this process. It is a very emotional time for all concerned.

Burial at sea

While burial at sea is rare and extremely expensive, some people with very close links with the sea-faring organisations may request to have their ashes scattered on the water.

Funeral Directors

Death is the stock in trade of funeral directors and, as we go about our daily lives, we generally give little thought to the service they provide. Undertakers have a practical approach to death, but they are conscious of the need to serve the public in a considerate, yet business-like manner. For the most part this is exactly what they do. **The Irish Association of Funeral Directors** (IAFD) have drawn up a charter for those who use their services and have even organised a complaints procedure for those who feel that the service they received was not up to the standard they expected. Details are available from funeral directors' offices and may also be found in the Golden Pages or Yellow Pages directories.

CHAPTER 15

Organ donation

Modern medicine

There have been many significant advances in medical science in the last one hundred years. The vision and dedication of very many scientists and medical practitioners has helped to increase the lifespan of many who would otherwise die. The pioneering work of Dr Christiaan Barnard in South Africa, for example, led to the first successful heart transplant in 1967. Nowadays such procedures are not only common but generally very successful. The various organs which currently may be transplanted are the corneas of the eyes, the heart, the lungs, the liver and the kidneys. The consistently most successful transplants are those of the cornea, simply because this part of the body has no blood supply, therefore there is no risk of rejection caused by blood-borne antibodies.

The loss of a loved one is tragic and traumatic and the heartbreak of seeing their dead body can be almost too much to bear. It is not surprising, therefore, that when we are caught up in our own grief that we might find it difficult to consider the thought of their body being cut up, even for a postmortem. The next of kin may be so consumed by grief at their recent loss that hospital medical staff are reluctant to intrude and request that consent for organ donation be given. Bodily organs die at different rates and must be harvested for donation as soon as possible. Hence the need to approach the bereaved so soon after the person has died.

How long do organs survive?
The tissues of the brain die within five minutes of death, while the heart tissues last for fifteen minutes and the kidneys survive for up to half an hour. These organs can be preserved for longer, however, if the dead donor is kept on a respirator. Corneas can be preserved for a much greater time in what is known as the eye bank.

Yet, more and more people are coming to the realisation that their loss could be someone else's gain; that the gift of life, or a better quality of life, could be given to others as a direct result of the death of their loved one. **The Irish Kidney Association** has been at the forefront in raising awareness about organ donation. It is surprising, that in spite of all the publicity surrounding the benefits from organ donation, that there is always such a shortage of organs for potential recipients. There have been suggestions from some quarters, particularly in the UK that it should be considered ethical to harvest suitable organs without the consent of the deceased's next of kin. Currently, no-one can be forced to donate a loved one's organs – even if the person had signed a donor card. If the next of kin do not want a donor's wishes to be carried out they have the option of refusing permission.

Parents for Justice

A new group, called Parents for Justice, has been set up to support the parents of those children who died in hospital and whose organs/tissue may have been retained. A list of confidential helplines can be found in Appendix 2.

CHAPTER 16

Practical issues after a death

Registering a death

When a person dies his or her death must be registered. Registration is made within whatever district of the Registrar of Births and Deaths the death occurs. A medical certificate stating the cause of death must be obtained from the doctor who attended the dead person. The person registering the death must present the medical certificate and sign the register in the presence of the registrar. There is no charge for registering a death, but there is a fee for the death certificate which can then be issued.

Persons eligible to register a death are the deceased's nearest relatives who were present at the death or during the final illness, or who are living in the district. Other persons present at the death may also register the death, as may hospital or nursing home staff or a funeral director.

Death grants / Compensation

When a person dies the family or next of kin may apply for a death grant which will help towards funeral expenses. In the twenty-six counties an additional bereavement grant of £1,000 is now available to widowed persons with dependent children. This grant is based on

PRSI contributions.

According to the Civil Liability Act, if a person dies because of the negligence of another, then the members of the family affected are entitled to compensation. A solicitor can advise regarding those entitled to claim, the procedure for doing so, and the amount of compensation likely.

If a person dies as a result of a prescribed occupation, a disease or an accident at work, then a survivor's allowance or compensation may be payable under the Occupational Injuries Benefit Scheme. Only one grant is payable, by cheque, to the spouse/partner/next of kin/personal representative of the deceased. Details of how to qualify can be obtained from the local Social and Family Affairs office or directly from the Death Grants Section, Government Buildings in Longford or local DHSS offices in Northern Ireland.

If a family has no income, a basic payment is available. Financial assistance, payable directly to a funeral director, may be available towards the cost of the funeral. The Health Board may provide a contract funeral when there is no next of kin or they cannot be found or they have no resources.

Pensions and other benefits
A contributory pension or non-contributory pension may be available to the surviving spouse/partner. Surviving children may be entitled to an orphan's allowance or orphan's contributory pension or orphan's non-contributory allowance. Certain extra benefits and/or concessions may be available depending on the age of

the surviving spouse. Extra tax free allowances are available to a surviving spouse in the year of the death and subsequently a widow/er's tax allowance applies. If there are dependent children, then one-parent family allowance may be available.

PLEASE NOTE

Allowances and benefits are available as of right. They are not charity. You should claim all the benefits to which you are entitled. **Don't be afraid to ask!**

There are **Citizens' Advice Centres** throughout the country. These services are free and confidential and a range of advice is offered on entitlements, taxation, allowances, benefits and other information.

Your local Community Welfare Officer can provide a range of information also. Local telephone numbers for these agencies can be found in the Golden Pages and Yellow Pages directories.

CHAPTER 17

Taking out insurance

Fear of death
One of our most basic instincts is that of self-preservation. Fear of death, therefore, is a completely natural response. Even with the firmest conviction in an afterlife, there are very few people who are totally unafraid of death. It is not surprising then, that we tend to avoid thinking or talking about it. Yet, it is reasonable that while we are in good health that we should confront our fears, albeit temporarily, and put our affairs in order.

We can do this by taking out a Life Assurance Policy and making a will. Some people might even choose to organise a pre-paid funeral plan for themselves. These practical actions are not going to hasten our death. They are simple, thoughtful arrangements, which will be of immense comfort to those who may be caring for us in our last days or indeed if we die sooner than expected.

Life Assurance Policies
The insurance industry has recently highlighted the fact that many homemakers are either under-insured or not insured at all. Life assurance companies have general guidelines for the cost of insuring risks. If you

apply for a Life Assurance Policy you can expect to undergo a medical examination. This is necessary so that the risk on your life can be assessed and your premium payments set accordingly. If you are a smoker or engage in risky activities such as mountain climbing or parachuting, then obviously your life is at greater risk than a person who does not engage in activities like these. Your age and sex will also be taken into account, as will your general health.

It is recommended that your policy should cover you for up to five times your annual salary. So if you are earning £20,000 per year then you should insure yourself for at least £100,000. While this may seem a large amount, given today's low interest rates, your family or next of kin could not expect to get much of an income by way of interest on this sum.

If you intend to take out a mortgage you are required by the lender providing the mortgage, to insure your life for the amount borrowed. Mortgage protection insurance will mean that if you die before the mortgage has been repaid then the lender will be guaranteed a return and your estate will be guaranteed the value of your property. So, if you borrowed £70,000 for a house five years ago and took out a mortgage protection policy for that amount, the property might now be worth £150,000 and this amount will add significantly to the value of your estate.

Inheritance tax
People who have a lot of money, valuable property or who run big businesses will be aware that the

beneficiaries of their estate may be liable for inheritance tax. Some insurance companies now provide policies which can act like mortgage protection and cover the amount of inheritance tax which will fall due after they die. Such policies can be index-linked but they cannot be cashed in as they have no surrender value.

CHAPTER 18

Making and executing a will

What is a will?

A will is a legal document in which you state how you wish your property to be divided after you are dead. Those who benefit from a will are called beneficiaries. A spouse and dependant children have certain entitlements automatically under the Succession Act and most people making a will provide appropriately and adequately for their spouse and surviving children. If this has not been done, those who feel aggrieved must be given notice by the executor/administrator of the will. This is so that they can assert their rights through the courts.

What is intestacy?

If someone dies without having made a will he or she is intestate and there are certain rules laid down by law for dealing with intestacy. The nearest surviving relative of the deceased, the one who is entitled to most of the estate, is entitled to apply for Letters of Administration, although this person may choose to defer to another family member or to a solicitor. According to the Succession Act the deceased's family will be entitled to a certain proportion of the estate, but it can take quite some time, much more than when there is a will, before everything is sorted out. If there are no surviving relatives, the government, through the probate office, can claim all of the estate.

Realty and personalty

A person's estate is what is left of his or her belongings after all liabilities and debts have been settled. Many people think that they don't actually have anything to leave, but a person's estate might include a house and lands (known as realty), and other personal property, any savings and life insurance policies, shares and investments, among other things (all known as personalty).

The role of the executor

If an executor has been appointed he or she must follow certain procedures in order to execute the will. If the executor does not wish to instruct a solicitor, then he or she may make a personal application to the Probate Office in the Four Courts in Dublin or to one of the fourteen district Probate Registries around the country.

Where there are no complications with the will or intestacy, sorting everything out should be reasonably straightforward. Where there are any complications, for example a partial intestacy (where the deceased did not bequeath all of the estate), then legal advice is essential.

The role of the administrator

If, when the will was made, no executor was appointed or if the executor was already dead, then an administrator must be appointed. As with an intestacy, the nearest surviving relative of the deceased, the one who is entitled to most of the estate, is entitled to apply for Letters of Administration.

In order to execute the will an executor must get a Grant of Probate. An administrator cannot get a Grant of Probate, instead they must obtain a Grant of Administration. Essentially they are both obtaining legal permission in order to divide the dead person's estate.

THE EXECUTOR OR ADMINISTRATOR MUST:

- Establish that they have the right to act in this capacity.
- Prove that the will (if there is one) is valid, in the Personal Applications Section of the Probate Office.
- Gather all information relating to the estate, calculate the total value and pay all outstanding debts.

Procedures for probate are similar in the twenty-six counties and in Northern Ireland. Probate personal application forms and explanatory leaflets are available by writing to or telephoning the **Probate Office**. This form must be fully completed and returned. An acknowledgement will be issued and a preliminary appointment will be made shortly afterwards. At least two appointments with the probate officers will be required.

FIRST APPOINTMENT

The following information is required by the probate officials at the preliminary appointment:

- Proper identification such as a passport, the death certificate and the original will.

- Full details of the person's estate and details of all accounts of any kind along with letters from the various banks and/or institutions confirming the balance of the accounts plus any interest accrued up to the date of death.
- Details of all life assurance policies, superannuation schemes or gratuities, and details of all stocks and shares, prize-bonds and cash. (Pensions to a spouse are not included.)
- Title deed or land certificates held by the deceased and a reasonable estimate of the value of the deceased's property (house or car) and the resale value of the contents of the house at the date of death.
- A list of all the deceased's debts. These might include any outstanding mortgage, personal loans and funeral expenses.

Note: The personal applicant may attend the preliminary appointment even if all these details are not available. Outstanding details can be given at the second appointment.

BEFORE THE SECOND APPOINTMENT

When a person dies, their tax affairs must be put in order so that the estate can be settled. After the preliminary appointment with the Probate Office and before the second appointment the executor/administrator will be required to:

- Notify the deceased's Tax Office of the date of death and make a Tax Return on behalf of the deceased, sorting out any tax affairs up to the date of death.

- Pay any taxes due. In some, but not all cases, Probate Tax, Capital Acquisition Tax, Capital Gains Tax, Inheritance Tax or Discretionary Trust Tax may be due.

- Identify certain indexed exemption thresholds. (The officials of the Revenue Commissioners are expert in dealing with these.)

- Ensure that all taxes are duly paid before distributing any legacies or entitlements, otherwise he or she may be held personally liable.

- Submit tax affidavit(s) for certification to the Capital Taxes Office of the Revenue Commissioners. The certified tax affidavit will be required by the Probate Office before a Grant of Representation can be issued.

If the estate is straightforward and uncomplicated, then a personal executor/administrator can work out the details with the relevant authorities. The professional help of an accountant, tax advisor and/or a solicitor (or indeed all three) will prove invaluable if the will or estate is in any way complicated. Many wills and intestacies are never properly completed, simply because the executor/administrator didn't have the time or the experience to follow the procedure required by law.

SECOND APPOINTMENT

- Bring all outstanding details and any other information required by the Probate Official.

- Present the certified tax affidavit(s) to the Probate

Office in order to get a Grant of Probate or a Grant of Administration.

- Sign the completed papers prepared on the basis of all the information supplied and swear an oath to the accuracy and truth of the contents.
- Pay a probate fee, calculated on a sliding scale. Currently the fees due for an estate valued at £200,000 are £240 in Republic of Ireland and £500 in Northern Ireland.
- When Letters of Administration are being sought, an independent surety or guarantor (who must be a resident of the country and be worth at least the value of the estate) is required and he or she must attend this appointment.
- All details will usually be completed at the second meeting, but the witnesses to the will may be interviewed.
- A Deed of Assent must be executed by the personal representative where real or leasehold property is to be transferred into the names of the beneficiaries. The services of a solicitor usually will be required for this.
- Once the Grant of Probate or Grant of Administration has been given, the executor/administrator may then convert the assets to cash to pay out any bequests or entitlements.

In a case where the death certificate includes senility as one of the causes of the deceased person's death it is necessary for the family physician who attended the person throughout their lifetime to swear an affidavit that the deceased was of sound mind at the time the will was made. Once this is done, the Grant of Probate can be assigned.

Writing your own will — don't

Will forms are available for a few pence in stationers and it is very easy to write your own will. But it also very, very easy to make an absolute mess of it in the process. It makes no sense at all to save a few pounds by going-it-alone and ending up causing major hassle and expense for those trying to execute the will after your death. A qualified solicitor will have the expertise to write your will exactly the way you want and have it totally legal. The cost will be well worth it – even just for peace of mind. It is also worth noting that from time to time, depending on Corporate sponsorship, certain members of the legal profession offer a free, or almost free, will-making service. Donations are made to charity for every will written.

Who gets what?

When someone dies, among the least savoury of emotions which come to the surface is avarice. 'Who's going to get what?' 'I was promised this!' 'You weren't told you could have that!' If a person has a favourite watch or other item of jewellery and wishes a certain member of the family to have it after his or her death, then this should be specified. Wills do not have to be immensely complicated. In fact the simpler the document, the better. If someone makes a will, then no one can be in any doubt as to who should get what! A proper, legally-binding will may be contested, but the likelihood of the case succeeding is rather slim.

Using a solicitor

Any person appointed as executor to a will may choose to instruct a solicitor. This will not be essential if the will is straightforward. However a person who is appointed as administrator of an estate where no will was made (intestacy) would be well advised to employ the services of a solicitor to take over the duties. It used to be the case that, for a fee, some insurance companies would provide, a bond of administration to members of the general public in order to protect against liabilities. It seems that such bonds are now only available to solicitors.

There are standard fees for probate and administration work which are levied on the gross value of the estate. The fees payable by solicitors to the Probate Office are half those paid by a personal applicant.

Currently solicitors fees for executing or administrating a will stand at:

3.5% on the first £10,000

3.0% on the next £10,000

2.5% on the balance

This does not include expenses outlay or V.A.T. @ 21%

In Northern Ireland rates for fees are available from solicitors on an individual basis. In general, two fees (based on the net value of the estate) are payable to the Northern Ireland Probate Office when personal applications are made.

These fees might appear to be a lot of money, but for some executors/administrators the legwork and paperwork are just too much of a headache, and handing over the lot to an experienced solicitor is worth anything. The stated fees do not include any litigation if there is a legal challenge to the will. Nor do they cover the cost of conveyancing fees or stamp duty if a property is transferred into the name of a beneficiary. This is usually paid by the person who benefits from the will.

It would be reasonable for the executor to discuss employing a solicitor with the family before proceeding, and solicitors are quite happy to discuss fees before starting the process at all. It makes for a much more satisfactory outcome all round if everyone is clear about the expenses involved in executing the will.

The executor/administrator may also consult with the family about disposing of the deceased's personal belongings which have not been willed. Clothes and small items such as photos can have a sentimental value for certain family members and considerable tact may be required to achieve a satisfactory outcome.

Making a will makes sense

Any person with money or any property of value should make a will. If for no other reason than to stop the government or other agencies getting a greater share of the assets than is necessary when that person dies. So make a will and make it soon! Making a will shows consideration for those left behind.

111

Appendix 1

BELIEF CENTRES

Bahá'í Faith, National Assembly of Ireland
24 Burlington Road, Dublin 4.
Tel: 01–6683150

Baptist (Calvary Bible Baptist Church)
23 Sefton Road, Rochestown Avenue, Dunlaoghaire,
Co. Dublin.
Tel: 01–2857344

Buddhist Centre
Kilmainham Well House, 56 Inchicore Road, Dublin 8.
Tel: 01–4537427

Catholic Press & Information Office,
169 Booterstown Avenue, Blackrock, Co. Dublin.
Tel: 01–2885043

Church of Ireland Communications Office
12 Darglewood, Dublin 16
Tel: 01–4935405

Humanist Association
25 Wolfe Tone Square West, Bray, Co. Wicklow.
Tel: 01–2869870

Islamic Cultural Centre
19 Roebuck Road, Clonskeagh, Dublin 14.
Tel: 01–2603740

Jehovah's Witnesses
Watchtower House, Newcastle, Co. Wicklow.
Tel: 01–2810692

Jewish Community Offices
Office of the Chief Rabbi, Dublin 6.
Tel: 01–4923751

Lutheran Church of Ireland
Luther House, 24 Adelaide Road, Dublin 2.
Tel: 01–6766548

Methodist Church
Abbey Street, Dublin 1.
Tel: 01–8742123

Mormons (Church of Jesus Christ of Latter-day Saints)
The Willows, Finglas Road, Glasnevin, Dublin 9.
Tel: 01–8306899

Quakers (Religious Society of Friends)
Swanbrook House, Morehampton Road, Dublin 4.
Tel: 01–6683684

Appendix 2

GENERAL INFORMATION CENTRES

Bereavement Grant / Death Benefit
Social Welare Office, Ballinlee Road, Longford.
Tel: 043–45211
Tel: 01–7043473

Central Tax Information Office
For General Information on Income Tax, including Capital Gains Tax, VAT and Corporation Tax.
Tel: 01–8780000

City Coroner's Court (Dublin)
Store Street, Dublin 1.
Tel: 01-8746684
Fax: 01-8742840

Coroner's Office (Belfast)
The Courthouse, Crumlin Road, Belfast BT14 6AL.
Tel: 080–1232–743040

Department of Health and Children
Hawkins House, Dublin 1
Tel: 01–6354000
Fax 01–6354001
e-mail: queries@health.irlgov.ie
website: www.doh.ie

The General Register Office (Dublin)
For information on registration of Deaths, Births,
Marriages, Adoptions and Stillbirths.
8 Lombard St. East, Dublin 2.
Tel: 01-6711863
Fax: 01-6354440

The General Register Office (Belfast)
Oxford House, 49 Chichester Street, Belfast BT1 4 HL.
Tel: 080–1232–252000

Health Boards
See local directory for further information on local
offices.

Injury Benefit
Social Welfare Office, 151/164 Townsend Street, Dublin 2.
Tel: 01–8748444

Organ Retention — Confidential Helplines
Our Lady's Hospital, Crumlin
Tel: 01–4096915 and 01–4096552
Eastern Health Board
Tel: 1800–670700
North Eastern Health Board
Tel: 1800–333033
Midlands Health Board
Tel: 1800–216101
Western Health Board
Tel: 1800–638888

North Western Health Board
Tel: 1800–200056
South Eastern Health Board
Tel: 1800–300655
Southern Health Board
Tel: 1800–742000
Midwestern Health Board
Tel: 061–482482

Pensions Services Office
College Road, Sligo
Tel: 071–69800
Tel: 01–8748444

Pensions Branch
Castle Court, Royal Avenue, Belfast BT1 1DF
Tel: 080–1232–520520

Probate Offices
See local directory for further information on local offices.
Social Welfare Services Office
Government Buildings, Ballinlee Road, Longford.
Tel: 043–4521
Tel: 01–8748444

Social Security Benefit Shop
Castle Court, Royal Avenue, Belfast BT1 1DF.
Tel: 080–1232–336000

Appendix 3

USEFUL ORGANISATIONS

AIDS Alliance
53 Parnell Square West, Dublin 1.
Tel: 01–8733799
Fax: 01–8733174

Barnardos
Christchurch Square, Dublin 8.
Tel: 01–4530355
e-mail: barnardos@iol.ie
Website: www.barnardos.ie
18 St Patrick's Hill, Cork
Tel: 021–552100
e-mail: info@cork.barnardos.ie

Beginning Experience
(For those experiencing the loss of a spouse through
death, separation or divorce.)
Pauline: 044–35841
Paul: 01–4538207

The Bereavement Counselling Service
Dublin Street, Baldoyle, Dublin 13.
Tel: 01–8391766

Cluaiscint (for the suicide bereaved)
Tralee, Co. Kerry
Tel: 066–25932 (Mon–Fri 10.00–12.30)

The Compassionate Friends
Cavan 049–38436.
Cork 021–291892/364 695
Clare 065–20024
Dublin 01–8322197
Donegal 075–31493
Galway 091–752033
Limerick 061–453609
Nenagh 067–32675

CURA (Crisis Pregnancy Care Service)
South Anne Street, Dublin 2.
Tel: 01–6710598
Website: www.iol.ie/cura
With offices throughout the country

HEBER
c/o Irish Hospice Foundation
Tel: 01–6603111

Irish Association for Palliative Care
Marymount Hospice, Wellington Road, Cork.
Tel: 021–507110
Fax: 021–507110

Irish Cancer Society
5 Northumberland Road, Dublin 4.
Tel: 01–6681855
Fax: 01–6687599
Freephone: 1800–200 700
Helpline Callsave: 1850–606 060

Irish Friends of the Suicide Bereaved
PO Box 162, Cork.
Tel: 021–294318

Irish Hospice Foundation
9 Fitzwilliam Place, Dublin 2.
Tel: 01–6765599
Fax: 01–6765657

Irish Hospice Foundation Bereavement Service
Our Lady's Hospice, Harold's Cross, Dublin 6W.
Tel: 01–4972101
Fax: 01–4972714
website: www.ourladyshospice.com
St Francis' Hospice, Station Road, Raheny, Dublin 3.
Tel: 01–8327537

Irish Kidney Association
Donor House, 156 Pembroke Road, Dublin 4.
Tel: 01–6689788
Fax: 01–6683820

Irish Stillbirth and Neo-natal Death Society (ISANDS)
Carmichael House, 4 Brunswick Street North, Dublin 7.
Tel: 01–8726996

Irish Sudden Infant Deaths Association (ISIDA)
See Carmichael House (above)
Tel: 01–8747007
Helpline Callsave: 1850–391 391
e-mail: isida@nsr.iol.ie
www.iol.ie/~isida

ISPCC
Head Office, 20 Molesworth Street, Dublin 2.
Tel: 01–6794944
e-mail: ispcc@ispcc.ie
Childline Freephone: 1800–666 666

Life — Pregnancy Care Service
29 Dame Street, Dublin 2.
Tel: 01–6798989
Fax: 01–6790694
Tel: 080–1232–241414 (Belfast)
Helpline Callsave: 1850–281 281

Miscarriage Association
See Carmichael House (above)
Tel: 01–8725550

National Sudden Infant Death Register
Georges Hall, The Children's Hospital, Temple Street,
Dublin 1.
Tel: 01–8788455
Fax: 01–8787696
e-mail: kibnsidr@iol.ie

Natural Death Centre
20 Heber Road, London NW2 6AA, UK

Our Lady's Hospice
See Irish Hospice Foundation Bereavement Service

Rainbows — Bereavement Counselling for Children
Rainbows Ireland, Loreto Centre, Crumlin, Dublin 12
Tel: 01–4734175
Fax: 01–4734175
e-mail: rainbows@eircom.net

Royal College of Surgeons of Ireland
(Anatomy Department)
St. Stephen's Green, Dublin 2
Tel: 01–4022260
Fax: 01–4022355
e-mail: admin@rcsi.ie
Website: www.rcsi.ie

St Francis Hospice
See Irish Hospice Foundation Bereavement Service

Samaritans
112 Marlborough Street, Dublin 1.
Tel: 01–8727700
Helpline Callsave: 1850-609 090
With offices thoughout the country

Sólás — Bereavement Counselling for Children
See Barnardos
Tel: 01–4732110
e-mail: solas@barnardos.ie

TACA (Teachers Adopting Counselling Approaches)
c/o Drumcondra Education Centre, Dublin 9.
Tel: 01–8379799

Victim Support
Haliday House, 32 Arran Quay, Dublin 7.
Tel: 01–6798673
24-hour Freephone helpline: 1800–661 771
Missing persons Freephone helpline: 1800–616 617

Bibliography

RR = Recommended Reading   C = Children's Reading

Anatomy Act 1832, Royal College of Surgeons of Ireland, St. Stephen's Green, Dublin 2

RR   *A Precious Past, A Hopeful Future*, a leaflet on Sudden Infant Death Syndrome and Bereavement by ISIDA, 1994

C   *Badger's Parting Gifts*, Susan Varley, Picture Lions, 1992

RR   *Care of the Dying*, Dame Cicely Saunders, The Hospice Movement, 1960

Coroner's Act 1962, Government Publications Office, Molesworth Street, Dublin 2

Death and Dying, edited by Colm Keane, Mercier Press, 1995

RR   *Dancing With Life*, Fr Vincent Travers OP, St. Martin's Apostolate, Parnell Sq, Dublin 1

RR   *Dealing with a Death in the Family*, Sylvia Murphy, How To Books Ltd., 1997

Death and the Family, Peter Uhlenberg in *Family in Transition*, Arlene and Jerome Skolnick, Harper Collins, 1992

RR   *Death — Helping Children Understand*, a leaflet by Barnardos, 1996

Debrett's Guide to Bereavement, Charles Mosley, Headline Book Publishing, 1995

RR   *The Directory of Hospice and Specialist Palliative Care Services in Ireland*, a leaflet by the Irish

Association of Palliative Care, 1996

Dying, Professor John Hinton, Penguin, 1967

Experiences of Abortion, Denise Winn, Optima Books, 1988

Further along the Road Less Travelled, M. Scott Peck MD, Simon and Schuster, 1993

Homicide in Ireland 1972–91, Dr Enda Dooley, Government Publications Office, 1995

C   *I Carried You on Eagles' Wings*, Sue Mayfield, Scholastic Children's Books, 1987

RR *The Irish Association for Counselling Directory — Guide to Counselling and Therapy*, Wolfhound Press, 1995

RR *Last Rights — Death, Dying and the Law in Ireland*, Patrick Hanafin, Cork University Press

Law in the Republic of Ireland — An Introduction, Richard Grimes and Patrick Horgan, Wolfhound Press, 1988

Laying Down the Law — A Practical Guide, Olive Brennan, Oak Tree Press, 1991

RR *Life After Loss*, Christy Kenneally, Mercier Press, 1999

RR *A Little Lifetime*, a leaflet on Stillbirth and Neonatal Death by ISANDS

Living Our Dying — Reflections on Mortality, Joseph Sharp, Rider Books, 1997

Living with Death — Activities to help children cope with difficult situations, Mary Jane Cera, Good Apple Publications, 1991

On Becoming a Counsellor, Eugene Kennedy and Sara C. Charles, Gill and Macmillan, 1990

Management of Terminal Illness, Dame Cicely Saunders, The Hospice Movement, 1978

Medicine Through Time, Joe Scott, Holmes and McDougall, 1987

RR   *Mortally Wounded*, Michael Kearney, Marino Books, 1996

RR   The Narnia Series (especially *The Magician's Nephew* and *The Lion, the Witch and the Wardrobe*, C. S Lewis, Harper Collins, 1999

RR   *The New Natural Death Handbook*, Edited by Nicholas Albery, Gil Elliot and Joseph Elliot of The Natural Death Centre, Rider Books, 1997

RR   *Necessary Losses*, Judith Viorst, Fawcett Gold Medal, 1986

RR   *On Death and Dying*, Elizabeth Kübler–Ross, Collins Macmillan, 1969

Religious Education at the Primary Stage, Ralph Gower, Lion Educational, 1990

RR   *Report of the National Task Force on Suicide 1998*, Government Publications Office, 1998

Surviving Adolescence, Peter Bruggen and Charles O'Brian, Faber and Faber, 1986

RR   *Swimming Against The Tide — Feminist Dissent on the Issue of Abortion*, Angela Kennedy, Open Air, 1997

The Coroner's Court — Dispelling the Myths, Dr. Brian J Farrell in *The St. Paul Medical Indemnity Scheme Newsletter,* Spring 1998

The Courage to Grieve, Judy Tatelbaum, Vermillion, 1997

The Life Project, Barbara Blackburn, Ligouri Publications, 1995

The Penguin Book of Childhood, edited by Michael Rosen, Penguin, 1995

RR *The Role of the Coroner in Death Investigation*, The Coroner's Court, Dublin 1, 1998

RR *The Samaritans Information Pack*, The Samaritans, 112 Marlborough Street, Dublin 1

The Tibetan Book of Living and Dying, Sogyal Rinpoche, Harper, 1992

RR *Way to Go*, Alan Spence, Phoenix/Orien Books Ltd, 1998

RR *What To Do About Tax When Someone Dies — A guide for personal representatives, beneficiaries, surviving spouses and trustees*, Revenue Commisssioners, 1998

RR *When Someone Dies — A Handbook of Adult and Child Bereavement,* a leaflet produced by the Medical Social Work Department, Beaumont Hospital, Dublin, 1998

RR *The Unknown Region — Inspirations on Living and Dying*, Eileen Campbell, Harper Collins, 1993

Your Guide To Irish Law, Mary Faulkner, Gerry Kelly and Padraig Turley, Gill and Macmillan, 1993